PUSHKIN PRESS CLASSICS

BACKGROUND FOR LOVE

'Some books you don't read, you experience.
This story of a woman who discovers
the full extent of her strength of will in a
sparkling summer of love, is one of them'
DIE WELT

'A fast-paced, highly intense, emotionally
gripping, autobiographical novel'
BUCHKULTUR

T0343774

HELEN WOLFF (1906–1994) was born in Macedonia to a German father and Austro-Hungarian mother. At twenty-one, she went to Munich to apprentice at Kurt Wolff Verlag, now remembered as Kafka's original publisher. She began an affair with Kurt Wolff, whom she would go on to marry. The couple fled Nazi Germany first for France and eventually for the United States, where they arrived almost penniless in 1941.

The Wolffs founded a new imprint of Pantheon Books there in 1942. Helen, a gifted linguist who could read in four European languages, published a wide range of significant works by writers including Italo Calvino, Umberto Eco, Georges Simenon and Boris Pasternak. She wrote fiction and plays but always kept her own writing private. *Background for Love* was first published in Germany in 2020 to wide acclaim.

MARION DETJEN is a historian at Bard College Berlin, where she teaches migration history and is director of the Program for International Education and Social Change, a scholarship program for displaced students.

TRISTRAM WOLFF writes and teaches English and Comparative Literature at Northwestern University.

JEFFERSON CHASE is the translator of some 40 books from German, including works by Thomas Mann, Volker Ullrich and Wolfgang Schivelbusch. He lives in Berlin.

BACKGROUND FOR LOVE

HELEN WOLFF

TRANSLATED FROM THE GERMAN
BY TRISTRAM WOLFF

EDITED AND WITH AN ESSAY
BY MARION DETJEN
TRANSLATED FROM THE GERMAN
BY JEFFERSON CHASE

PUSHKIN PRESS CLASSICS

Pushkin Press
Somerset House, Strand
London WC2R 1LA

Original text © 2022 The Estate of Helen Wolff
English translation © 2024 Tristram Wolff
Essay original text © 2022 Marion Detjen
Essay English translation © 2024 Jefferson Chase

Background for Love was first published as
Hintergrund für Liebe by Weidle Verlag, 2020

First published by Pushkin Press in 2024
This edition first published in 2025

The translation of this book was supported by a
grant from the Goethe-Institut

1 3 5 7 9 8 6 4 2

ISBN 13: 978-1-80533-074-5

Designed and typeset by Tetragon, London
Printed and bound in the United Kingdom by Clays Ltd, Elcograf S.p.A.

www.pushkinpress.com

CONTENTS

BACKGROUND
FOR LOVE

This is it: we're really on our way. Blankets and big suitcases and coats, a pile of maps, sunglasses to protect us from the dust and the glare. Chocolate, hard-boiled eggs, cognac, bananas: it's going to be a long journey, a journey without lunch, instead we'll have a quick bite when the gates are lowered at railroad crossings, and there'll be irritated chewing when we're delayed at the border.

We've put a long winter behind us, full of work and anxieties, rain, fog, hail and snow. It's five in the morning. We have the feeling we're running from something, toward the easy life, toward a sunlit world. It's almost a kind of betrayal, this journey through the gray morning haze, betrayal of the friends who have stayed behind to freeze, betrayal of the morning and evening papers that from now on will only ever reach us late, hardly any scent left to them, hardly even true anymore. We feel guilty as Germany slips by beneath us, devoured by our accomplice's four wheels, as the windshield wiper, eager accessory, busily shoves away a fine mist of rain.

We're on our way: the car, you and I.

Oh yes, in spite of it all it's sheer joy to be on the road. Anything could happen to us, a flat tire, an accident might call us back, like a gendarme hard on the heels of a fugitive—but each kilometer makes us feel safer. The uncertain early light grows surer, more confident. We really are on our way—

I move closer to you. You wear thick gloves, a good camel traveling coat, you're hidden in its warm skin and you watch your turns closely, you watch for slippery streets and for obstacles that might get in the way of your progress. Later on it will get easier, I know, clearer, your strained attention can relax once the world crosses from the early hour into plain morning, the spell broken. But at this hour shrubs still look like haycarts, haycarts like shrubs, danger lurks, the farmers have long poles on the sides of their carts hidden by the early light. We have to just keep going, we can't afford to get tripped up now, we're on our way.

'It's gorgeous,' I say. 'Not completely real yet.'

The car veers sharply to one side. A prehistoric creature lumbers against us, bangs and clatters past.

'We could have been killed,' you say.

'You should have used the horn.'

'At this hour?'

The roads are an adventure, like a jungle. Something could be lying in wait round any corner, ready to leap out at us. But we love adventure, we surrender to its winds as they come at us over the radiator.

'Annemarie said to me, how can you go to that fashionable, crowded seaside—'

'Just wait.'

I sink into silent exhilaration. We count kilometers and calculate hourly averages. You tell me about the wide, long, straight avenues in France—*tout droit, tout droit, comme un billard, Madame*—the mottled trunks of plane trees to the right and left. We talk about the journey and not us, though here too we are marking a departure from old habits for new. Up till now we've met for meals together, been to concerts together, danced with each other, talked deeply, fought and loved each other. You are familiar to me from those many hours; but how you look while shaving, that I don't know. I'm still not acquainted with your morning mood or your working quiet; I only know your exceptions, not your rules. This trip is meant to lead us to common ground, we want to weather new adventures, different from the old. We're no longer challenging each other to small war and small peace, we are braving the dragon called *every day* that dwells in the cavern *every night*. How long until I've exhausted all my reserves, everything I've read or can remember, until I won't be able to enchant you with words anymore because you'll know all of mine already. And you'll notice how quickly I get tired, and—but I'm not afraid of what *I'll* notice.

'What are you thinking?'

No, I don't tell you what I'm afraid of. 'How many kilometers to the border?'

'Take a look at the map.'

I get the map out. I comb over it for the villages and towns and can't find the road. Finally I find it, but can't add up the distance in kilometers. I fall in your esteem. You tell me to take the wheel. No, I am no Diana on these country roads, no bold knight of the steering wheel, you've found me out too soon. I daydream easily and see trees instead of milestones, rooftops instead of signposts. If you've taken me for competent—

'What are you thinking?'

'I'm wondering whether we'll find a cottage.'

'Wouldn't we be better off in a hotel? It's much more comfortable.'

'Everyone lives in hotels. No, it has to be a cottage. And it should stand in a small meadow and a white cat should sit on the well and purr as soon as you look at her. And I want a fig tree in front of the doors, then we'll want to grow old like Philemon and Baucis and never go back to Munich or Berlin.'

'Of course,' you say seriously, and step on the gas, now that the road is straight and widening. 'Yes. Never again. Not until fall.'

He said until fall, I think: that could be September or November. But I don't ask. Until fall is a long time, more than just months, more than a quarter of a year. With a few words you've cut a fat slice out of the round year and put it on my plate. I look wonderingly, because it's still whole, only the crumbs of an hour have fallen off it.

Meanwhile, because the day is now bright, you place your arm round me and drive with only your left hand. I'm lost in admiration.

We are free. We are happy. We have money for a few months, you more, I less, as is the way with us. I'm nearly certain that you love me and that it can last perhaps for a summer. Especially in the south, where they say it's in the air. Yes—step on the gas pedal, cut into the fog and rain, soon we'll be in Switzerland.

Already we're at Lake Constance, and here and there you can see trees blossoming.

One border guard asks us how much money we have and whether we don't in fact have more. Another wants to see our car's registration number, to know how much tobacco we have, how many cigarettes. The car rattles impatiently, because you can't bring yourself to turn the motor off. The tollbooth attendants are wet and freezing and show some understanding. They grasp at least that we have to keep moving, that already another country is opening up for us.

It's welcoming here, it's peaceful. But we hardly take it in. We can't stop for the gorgeous blue lakes of Zürich, Vierwaldstadt, Geneva. We don't stop to rest in the surrounding villages. It's beautiful, but we drive past and the landscape doesn't sink in. Only small fragments, scraps of mountains, a pretty rising curve, all the flags on the hotels in Geneva. We've devoured all of Switzerland. The day grows tired like us, but you still want to get to France before it's over, drink warm red wine and sleep in a wide bed like you've promised.

We haven't spoken, haven't paused, only pushed on, onward, onward. You sit doggedly at the wheel and take the curves hungrily. The mountains to you are obstacles, you curse at the slower cars and want to clear the train crossings like hurdles. You only open your mouth when I stuff a hard-boiled egg or a banana into it, or when I entice you with a chicken leg. You don't look my way. But I know we're of one mind, we're silently fixed on the same goal, strung on the same bow, I'm grateful beyond words to have been brought along, to be allowed to sit mounted here alongside you. And while you gallop I hold on breathlessly, just as women have always clung full of joy and fear to the manes of horses bearing them away.

You're still wearing your winter face, rather furrowed, simultaneously tired and impatient, but a new skin is already growing underneath. Forty years old, I think, amazed: to have eaten your fill so many times and yet still be so hungry. To have seen so much, and still want to see more; loved so much, and yet be seduced again and again.

Out of the blue you say, 'Remind me I have to write to Eva, she always worries.'

This again. I'm brave and ask cheerfully: 'Why go off with me this time, anyway?'

'I want to spend a summer with you.'

'And with Adelheid?'

'Holy Week,' you respond, pleased with yourself. 'And now let's talk about today and tomorrow. Have you ever eaten bouillabaisse?'

No, I have not. I've seen absolutely nothing, eaten absolutely nothing interesting or exciting.

'You've run off with a virgin,' I say.

'We'll soon take care of that. This is France, after all.' You say this grandly, as though handing me the country on a serving platter.

Each country welcomes us with the same words of greeting: *Cigars—Cigarettes—Tobacco*. France is no exception. The customs agent is appealingly lazy. *Ça ira* becomes *ça va*, the republic consolidated. We're allowed to drive on and now all borders are behind us. In a deeper sense, we've arrived. Already the French country roads are all around us. They're not country roads at all, actually, but boulevards, absolutely straight and arched over with still-barren branches. The distance markers are adorned with red caps and they're numbered, *Route Nationale 201*—now even I can find my way—and we'll stay on this road until we reach Chambéry.

'Chambéry—a good place for truffles,' you instruct me. 'It's a crime to drive through truffle country without stopping, only excusable in this case because these aren't the *real* truffles. Those grow in Périgord.'

French place names fill the mouth wonderfully, there is something savory in their sound. We become bold. We forget the thunderclouds brewing back home in Germany. You talk about truffles and express a desire to drink a warm Châteauneuf du Pape this evening—these are the borders now to be crossed, a lust for life growing up from the earth. The billboards cry out, *Cointreau, Pernod*—Hitler and Hindenburg seem far away.

We hardly saw each other in the days leading up to our departure.

'How long has it actually been?' you ask.

'So long that I'm practically like new,' I say.

'Tonight,' you say.

But tonight you'll be tired, full of food and wine, and you'll want to rise early in the morning, so no, not tonight.

We kiss. Evening draws nearer. We plan to spend the night in Grenoble. Grenoble, by the Isère River, which flows to our left along the avenue. This is my first time in France. The roads are beautiful, the trees beautiful, one of divine creation, the other human, and it's good. I'd like very much to kiss you again, but the city's outskirts are busy with cyclists and you have to drive carefully to avoid them.

We quarrel fiercely over the hotel. You want to stay at the Majestic and I think it's too grand. At last we ask a policeman to referee the debate. We land at the Majestic.

This is France. Our room comes with a gigantic bed. It's a matchmaking hotel, I discover. No one asks for my name. *C'est la dame à Monsieur.* No one wants to know whether we're married; if what we want is to sleep together, all is well.

We freshen up. The windows are open wide, noise echoes up from the plaza below, some festival with a circus and carousel. You want to go down and take a look, have a go on the see-saw, but I'm too much diminished from the journey, unwillingly I confess I'm more fatigued than you. Then comes the food—the whole menu, actually. The waiter sets the chicken on the side table and we sit across from the giant bed and drink wine.

Now you tell stories about Monte Carlo. You get very animated and sketch out the gaming table and draw *rouge et noir, pair et impair, passe et manque.* My head spins like a roulette wheel, I say yes and nod and don't follow.

'The bank has better odds than the player,' you say. 'You see, when you roll a zero…'

You fill my glass. I'm not used to this much wine and it draws its circle around me, I feel like a stone dropped in water, now I'm sinking deep and then it lifts me back up lightly to the surface, where I stay buoyant, tipsy.

The waiter has cleared our dishes away. We're alone in a strange town, I haven't even seen it, it was already night when we arrived, I only know that Stendhal was born here: mere literary reminiscence, no more of that, just sit quietly.

'Time for bed—come here, I'll help with those clothes.'

'But I thought—I thought you still wanted to write a card.' While the bath is running you sit at the desk wearing a bath-towel and do in fact, remarkably, write a postcard, despite the hour. I'm in awe. Eighteen hundred kilometers at the wheel, plus the wine, but you can still write postcards—right now writing a postcard sounds like climbing the Matterhorn to me.

'Hmm,' you say, licking a stamp—yes, you've miraculously conjured French stamps from somewhere—'the card has to go out tonight. I really can't go downstairs like this. Would you?'

I walk the length of the hallway to the stairs apprehensively. Oh God—the stairs! They're horrifyingly wide, down the middle runs a narrow red strip. I'm to walk along this strip, it's clear, and the strip leads into the great hall, where everyone looks at you. It stretches like a tightrope. I think desperately of my guardian angel, wondering whether he's invisibly steadying me so I don't tumble onto the smooth white marble on my right and left. And all for Eva, I think, all these terrors for Eva, these awful trials for Eva. I'm filled with rage and suddenly I'm on solid ground, as a small attendant—there's my guardian angel—takes the card from me and sticks it into a narrow slot that's somehow both a little higher and a little lower than you'd expect. I marvel at this young page and the angel helps me on my way, I reach the elevator and go back up, emerge at the correct floor, now the final adventure: I have to choose the right door, then there you are, my love, and you've taken possession of the enormous wide bed, legs spread far apart: I hunt for a small corner to fold myself into, and see that you're already asleep.

And here we are at the end—the speedometer jumps from 100 to 110—behind us lies a foggy morning in the Savoie mountains, stone huts, destitution, barrenness, the gray of the stones and the inhabitants, herds of goats driven by young Savoyard boys, fond memories from the books of my childhood—and then the descent, gliding down into these blessed plains, into the first rays of sun, into an immaculate church-window blue, into the fertile expanse, into olive groves—so this is Provence—old, heavy and rich with history, aged and clarified in the cellar of many centuries, and always born anew under this sun. We drive past vineyards and rubble slopes, among strange rust-red domes of rock, moon-mountains you call them. The heavens stretch over us unbroken, colors glow more truly, houses and farms shimmer pink and ocher, cypresses and poplar rows stand upright against the wind, a stunning and severe drawing of the southern landscape.

Maybe there is no such thing as a fatherland, as they call it back home; and borders are arbitrary and that's why they're so often moved around, here as there; what there are instead are climates, milder and harsher, rougher and gentler, and climates kind to us humans.

You know the country here, you and our good steed, you've bathed in this world before, left the other far behind, cold, hard, gridded with laws. You drive past what's here too, further southward, until the last barrier in your path is gone; you wind through the Maritime Alps, and then you really give her free rein, poor heaving beast, the road pulls straight and wide once more, it glows white under the sun, you laugh, happy for the first time in months, you laugh as if you'd accomplished some victory, like someone who's conquered a country and rides in triumphant. The vernal blues of the sky stretch over you like triumphal arches, almond trees are holy virgins who curtsey as you pass but you hardly spare them a glance. '*Nice*'—you toss the name to me—and the wind snatches the word from your mouth, leaving it far behind. Already the city begins to show the tips of its toes, and now you hail the sea in greeting—which all of a sudden, at this magic word, comes into view, only to vanish again alluringly—you greet it like the Greeks: *Thalatta, Thalatta!*

'That was the most beautiful drive of my life,' I say.

We're sitting at Pistonato's on the Promenade des Anglais, and you order, very much at home here.

'You're still young,' you say. 'Now, we'll have the bouillabaisse and the *rosé du pays* with it   to a warm and beautiful summer to come, my dear child!'

'So you think it's beautiful too?'

'Yes, spectacularly so. With you. And tonight I won't fall asleep like yesterday, that was unforgivable.'

'Is it customary here to talk about making love over lunch?'

'It's the French way.'

Then I powder both our noses, mine first since that's more important, and we consider where to stay tonight.

'Nice,' you instruct—because you know everything, or just about everything, and you've tried everything too—'is a city for shopping, and for eating the best ice cream. Not for living, and not for making love.'

'Anyhow,' I say (I say 'anyhow' far too much, you tell me), 'it's a city. And the palm trees look like giant feather dusters.'

'You always manage to find a flaw,' you say.

'Always,' I say. 'Anyhow, I don't want to be in a city. What we wanted was to rent a cottage in a meadow.'

'Hmm,' you reply. 'Did we?'

At least you don't say no.

The bouillabaisse arrives, seasoned with saffron and garlic, swimming with hunks of bread soaked in broth, and among them float langoustines, fish with complicated names, mussels and onion slices. It's a bright, voluptuous dish, a dish for people who take joy in life.

'You should really have a mustache for this meal,' I say as you bite down on a langoustine shell. 'A good long mustache, so that both ends can drip slowly and deliciously. It's such wonderfully messy food, why don't you make more noise eating it?'

We smack our lips noisily. We slurp from langoustine shells till they're empty. We eat with Pantagruelian manners, the juice drips from our hands and mouths. One can only eat this way on the street under an awning, not surrounded by mirrors in some formal dining room—the sea and the sun don't mind a bit. Between courses we wash our hands. The next dish is artichokes. Once again we're a mess.

'How does the south strike you so far?' you ask during a break from this hard work.

'Blue,' I say, and reach for another artichoke, to really make the handwashing worth it. 'I love it, so long as I get to eat with my hands.'

'You haven't seen anything yet—nothing at all,' you say. 'But just around the corner there's lots more of the south to see; I think we'll need to go for a drive.'

'Do you really? Can that be true?' I ask.

'Today is Friday,' you say, 'so yes, it can be true.'

Friday is my day of good fortune. On Friday, everything is true.

A grubby man brings by astonishing carnations white as snow. You buy a bunch and lay them between us. We pretend to be on our honeymoon by the Mediterranean. You kiss me, and I blush.

'Everyone kisses on the street here,' you advise.

'At two in the afternoon?'

'Two in the afternoon is a very proper hour, as good as any other. Now, let's see if we can find a post office.'

In your language, to look for the post office means enough nonsense, back to reality, back to reason. You can never quite shrug off your restraints, never quite swing free in the present. Mail attaches you to the country and people you left behind with such impatience only yesterday. Even this climate isn't perfect. If I had Aladdin's magic lamp or at least his ring, I'd wish for part of this beautiful world to be elevated to a stratosphere where no postman could go, somewhere with a spell too strong for the telegraph operator to break.

Of course there's no post office. You're caught between relief and disappointment. I want to walk to the flower market. I'm impressed by the gorgeous bay, endless, pure, washed by the sea, nothing can ruin it, not even the casino. We've walked all along the quay by these absurd pink fountains and light fixtures which look—so you tell me—like lit-up bidets in a fancy brothel, and I must say it's how I would imagine a brothel might look. The world is divided into the precious blues of sky and ocean and the cheap pinks of these sugar sculptures, and humans can only sign the latter as their invention. And the humans themselves fit right in: groomed baboons and guinea fowl under their Basque-striped parasols, idle and chattering—but we don't stay long, and God likewise seems not to want to examine this place too closely, where Rolls-Royces are allowed to pile up to the sky.

I'm hanging on to your arm. I'm small and you're big. If I don't cling tightly I'll have to trot behind you, out of breath, like a little dog tied by a short leash to the back of a car.

The landscape, someone once said—a most charming woman—is best understood as a background for love. Here in this moment, when our strides are in sync, the foreground and background merge, the bay with your face, the warmth of the sun with the feeling of love, into complete relaxation, a weightless, suspended, intoxicating serenity; for just a few seconds life is perfect, humanity redeemed. You: you're more than a lover, you're the great enchanter, you make our dreams real. Other men offer tender words, other men are more faithful or at least love longer, but you are the one always looking for ways to leap from the everyday into the extraordinary, you don't let yourself get attached or settle. Other men are rational and intelligent, but they also have worries and doubts. Instead you have courage and wings. I love you as one loves a bird or some other beautiful, strong, light-hearted animal. In this instant I love you without reservation, set adrift from my own fate, which when I'm with you climbs to new heights, sublime and precarious. I love you as you are.

You look at me. You don't ask, as you usually would, what I'm thinking. You know. We mirror one another without a word, our images are clear. I imagine eternity is just like this moment. And in another moment, it's gone.

A yellow car stops suddenly and skillfully in front of us. Oh, not this: now for the routine and tedious *Where have you come from?—How long are you staying?* You greet the elegant woman behind the wheel, who suits the landscape so exactly, she looks like a great bouquet of pink carnations, she blossoms and carries a gay hat and is colorful all over, much too colorful for my taste, and all at once I'm painfully conscious of my paleness, my dirty overcoat, my not-so-new shoes and my very, very old beret. A person should look like a person, not a meadow in summer, I think, and I doubt the genuineness of her hair color even as I know in my heart it's real, but that doesn't improve my mood. The woman is kind, to me as well as you, overbearingly so I decide. It's too bad you can't just say to people: You're bothering us, dear woman, stop blocking our light, drive on, *adieu*, farewell!

But of course you're being kind now too, the two of you

toss questions back and forth, I grow impatient and scan the newspapers at the kiosk: corpse defilement, decision of the cabinet, exchange rate of the British pound, news in every language. Now go away—*va t'en*—off with you—

You go on chatting. Dear God, don't let him make plans with this woman, I pray, weakness of the pound, naval agreement, just give me this one day, maybe two—

You pull me over and hold my arm a little more tightly than necessary, which means 'Get a hold of yourself.'

'We're going to walk to Vogade for ice cream.'

We—which means the woman, you and me. On the way she learns this is my first time here.

'Oh, you mustn't run around without a hat in this sun, it's too much. You're already so pale.'

Only with great difficulty do I manage to keep her from putting her own hat on my head. She really is very kind. Suddenly she vanishes into a store and reappears with a parasol. It's a bit colorful, but I say thank you and you're touched. Then we sit outside at Vogade and eat ice cream, and you engage us—us—for the following morning. And in the afternoon we're supposed to go for tea at this woman's house, because somewhere around here she has one; and in the meantime I'm supposed to go hat-shopping with her since, of course, she knows the shops.

At last you announce it's time for us to go. We still intend to make it to Menton. Your farewell is prolonged and sincere. I keep mine brief and mute. I've left the parasol behind at Vogade. Unfortunately, you remind me in time.

'What a lovely, kind, attentive woman, very open-minded. If we spent the summer in this area, she could give us a few tips. Did you like her as well?'

'I'd call her hyperactive.'

You laugh. 'She's just healthy.'

'I've always shopped for my hats by myself,' I venture.

'And it shows, my dear.'

'Well I don't want to look like a tropical bird.'

'Are you jealous? So soon?'

How you ask it! As if jealousy were some disgusting disease, the lowest and most despicable thing you can catch. And with that you place yourself several rungs above me, lay pettiness and selfishness on my account, pre-empt every word or objection that might form on my lips.

Yes—maybe I am already jealous. But I really don't like this woman. I disliked her from the start, and I wouldn't have spent time with her of my own volition, here or anywhere else, with or without you. She's loud and she gets on my nerves, and she's nothing like any of my friends. You ought to have known this, grasped it, instead of applying your simple, comfortable masculine formula to every situation as usual, casting me from now on as the jealous woman.

I grow quiet. We drive down a fairy-tale road. You've already forgotten and are back in the present, point out Cap Ferrat to me with its lighthouse, Monte Carlo the operetta city, Èze the bird's nest in the steep cliffs, you point and you glow with the pleasure of seeing old friends, the pleasure of gift-giving, for it's you, yes you, bestowing this country on me. We both forget the blonde woman. Things are no longer perfect, but after all they're still very, very good.

We drive through Cap Martin without stopping, you promise we'll return there the day after tomorrow, gardens and olive groves, pine trees bent over the water—a background for love.

And then we're in Menton. The slanted roofs of the old city stand out darkly against the blue sky, charmingly crowded around a church-tower that rises up from the gorgeous arched bridges, brightly colored boats, and brown nets of the harbor, the bay curves gently round, and I can easily believe the Romans called it 'Peaceful Bay'.

The hotel recommended by our blonde friend is the sort of fine establishment that suits you, not me. We're booked into what amounts to a small apartment: two rooms, a bathroom and a tiny vestibule, all on the top floor at the end of a long hallway. I don't think we've ever been so secluded. We have a balcony higher than the palm trees growing in the front garden. I unpack your things, lay them out lovingly on the bathroom vanity, the army of brushes and combs, the small flasks and bottles, I lightly make fun of your packing—you *man of property*—we kiss on the balcony, and the sun goes down. You send telegrams so your mail will reach you here, you're surprised I have no messages to send, not so much as a postcard. And then I unpack my own things, everything a young bachelor woman needs: a large grip, an overnight bag. It's quickly emptied or filled again. It's ugly and convenient. When I want to leave in a hurry, we're both travel-ready in half an hour. Comb and brush, two small tins, two small bottles: my side of the vanity looks scanty, like it's been picked clean. And then I dress up proudly in my evening wear, still more or less in fashion, and I'm ready before you're even done shaving.

So this is how you look covered in shaving cream. And this is the way you walk through the room, mirror in hand, instead of sitting still like a dignified person. It seems there's no such thing as privacy to be had with you: you fling the door open without knocking, sit down on my bed and leave flecks of foam on the carpet, you search through my dresser, you are amazed that I have no perfume or skin cream, and I think how nice it is to have no privacy, no distance built into our closeness. I am half shocked, half enchanted. I throw you out and two minutes later am disappointed you're not back yet. You disappear for ten minutes and I feel abandoned. But then you reappear, bringing lipstick and rouge, suitable for a woman of the world now in the company of a man of the world who's left her practical, bread-earning days behind her.

I put on make-up while you offer advice. It seems you've watched other women with close attention. But I'm not thinking of other women just now. You're impatient and touched by my faltering, my lack of confidence. Suddenly you say, 'You really are the innocent,' and we kiss to test whether the lipstick is safe to kiss. I feel secure around you, I throw the past and future into the nearby sea, I decide to be at home in your arms and in this elegant hotel, not to be afraid in front of the doorman or the strangers in their evening wear, I'm slightly intoxicated and set free from myself. I find you beautiful, good, young, an excellent companion for adventure. I decide to live the good life this time, arm in arm we descend the stairs, cross the street to the restaurant dining room on the water, where naturally you get us a table by the window. The waves below us slap gently, a radio softly plays 'Happy Days', I see the lights of Menton, you see the lights of Ventimiglia, the moon is rising, you search out my foot under the table, the langoustines arrive and we're toasting one another when— 'Man'—a voice interrupts this scene; 'Man, what on earth are *you* doing here?'

I would happily have stabbed this voice, in fact I was already holding the knife, but you leap up, already beaming, a small man embraces you, he's dark-haired and tanned and has the energy and countenance of a little monkey. 'Man,' he says, 'this is fantastic.' I give him a look and lay the knife down again, he pulls a chair up to our table, sniffs like a dog at the breeze wafting around us, decides against politics or the economy and talks instead of wine, the countryside, women.

'See that woman over there?' he asks. 'An American, the doorman tells me, with a delicate, porcelain face, wears clothes in soft pastels, has a smile that could outlast Mona Lisa, only less secretive. I call her Keep Smiling. It's a funny thing, isn't it—love? For me it always comes on quick. There I am sitting on the beach, this woman thank God has a dog—'

'In the Renaissance dogs were the courtesan's companion,' you say. 'Just think of Titian.'

'These women have a talent for making nothing of marriage—really, I find it extraordinarily appealing.'

'How far along are you?' you ask.

'Man,' he says, 'you got here just in time. I need your advice, since you're something of a specialist when it comes to love. I've already met with her for tea once. That was nice, but we had no privacy. Now I want to take her out for an evening stroll. But—should I try for a kiss? Or should I walk her back to her room right away? Or—'

'I'd have a word with the doorman,' you say. 'Are you thinking of tonight for this walk?'

'One moment,' says the small man, and jumps up. Keep Smiling turns her smile up a notch. She plucks grapes from a bunch with meticulously manicured fingers. Every woman's eyes are on her table. The small man speaks in a low voice, confidentially.

'Bold,' I say.

'How do you like him?'

'Sweet,' I say. 'He could be our little son.'

The small man returns dissatisfied. 'Life is short and she's putting me off. Has to play bridge this evening. Bridge: the Anglo-Saxon substitute for having a love life. What an idiot nation, eh? They need civilizing—'

We return to the hotel. In the smoking parlor there's a slot machine. The coins go in at the top, you spin a wheel in the middle, then if all goes well ten times what you put in comes out at the bottom. But that almost never happens. The men try their luck—when have they ever been able to resist this sort of thing?—the small gentleman, his name is Erich, has lost twenty francs, and on your losses no comment. A pair of shoes, my calculating brain tells me; it thinks more easily in terms of the value of practical objects.

'I have an idea,' cries Erich, 'a wonderful idea. This piece of junk is a joke. Let's drive to Monte Carlo. We'll get square again there, for sure.'

And so we drive to Monte Carlo, squashed tightly together all three of us in the front of your car, in high spirits, adding our headlights to all the others illuminating the magical night. This outdated world lives on for who knows how much longer: the ghastly casino, the ghastly carpeting with recessed footlights, yet everything is crowded with people, with cars, with lights. I find it all uncanny, like murky water frothed up into foam: the uncanny casino, the uncanny monotonous noises, the uncanny fanatics, most of whom you seem to recognize and point out to us. The Zero-Freak, the Phosphorescent Man, the Drowned Body— nearly all stand to the side, haunting the tables, they jot down symbols and figures in notebooks, abracadabra, incantations for luck. The whole scene is otherworldly: the croupier's rake, the eerie roll of the ball, it's just what you always read about and it's all there, exactly as it's described in books. Here the world has stood still, it doesn't turn round its accustomed axis, it turns instead with a nightmarish monotony, with nightmarish sameness, in the same ghastly spaces under the same ghastly chandeliers, around scores of minuscule balls thrown by an indifferent hand. You call out rash, statistically derived numbers. I can only feel the stationary moment. Outside is the starry sky and soft breeze; in here, it's stifling and oppressive. My radiant mood is spoilt and suddenly you're both nowhere to be found.

You—yes you, you too are under the spell, I've never seen you like this, so unguarded, so greedy and almost mean. You've found a chair at last, you have a notebook out, you scribble and draw graphs, you move chips around feverishly, giving, taking, tossing, the larger ones as well that weigh more, worth a great deal of money. I place a hand on your shoulder, you spin round angrily and hiss at me. I go. I find a small bench against the wall meant for players who want to count their money. I sit down and let a few tears fall, cry and hate money, think of my overnight bag, hate you, hate this whole coast where once again before sunrise money and property, property and money enjoy this idolatry. A crowd forms around the table where you're playing. People are drawn as if by magic as soon as lots of money is being won or lost. The circle of onlookers doubles. My heart catches. You sit there, hoarse, sweat on your forehead, the veins on the backs of your hands are swollen and blue, you toss banknotes down on the table, you fling them desperately across the table's surface, no time even to exchange notes for tokens, the ball rolls and like a madman you keep throwing money, emptying wallet and coat pockets, a last few bills fly into the vortex. *Don't*, I cry, *don't*—but no human voice can reach you now, only the croupier's monotone. It lasts mere seconds, but I know during these seconds I could fall down dead and your heart would be unmoved. Zero, the croupier calls. You wipe the sweat from your brow, a handful of heavier tokens make their way back to you, you smile, turn round and, wearing a wrecked, aged, hunted face, your hands trembling, you say: 'Exactly even.'

'Man,' says Erich, 'Man—are you nuts, that was thirty thousand francs!'

No, I think, that was our entire summer you tossed down onto the table. That was it, our freedom, our long days unclouded by worry—

'I didn't win a sou, but if I'd lost I'd have lost sixty thousand francs.'

'But why on earth do something so idiotic?'

'It's the greatest thrill in this world,' you say. 'The second before the ball finds its number is like the last second between life and death. Life hangs by a hair, then fortune's stroke lands. The rush is incredible, it's a rush of fear, a feeling like nothing else.'

'You've got to be lucky,' mutters Erich. 'I never bet more than ten francs at a time, and I lost five hundred. And that was me showing restraint.'

'You've got to be daring, my friend,' you laugh, changing your tokens back into banknotes.

Erich inspects me and says: 'Our dear lady here is pale, she needs a cognac,' and he puts a solicitous arm through mine as you count your money.

Erich, with your snub nose like a small dog, you made your ten-franc bets so cautiously, I saw it. You were angry when they were taken from you, so you bet again, only to be annoyed again, in the meantime cursing, *Shit!* you said, and plenty of other things besides. You play roulette the way one plays marbles, your hands don't tremble, your heart stays uninvolved. Erich, you can still see that I'm pale, you're a human here among the possessed.

'Come on, man,' says Erich, 'let's get out of this stinking box, we have to go celebrate. I'm leaving a winner.'

'I thought you lost five hundred francs?'

'Listen, I've got a system. I designate a certain amount, and then I stick to it. I made myself a promise: don't lose more than a thousand francs at the tables. I've still got five hundred to lose. But the thing is I'm getting bored. So since I didn't lose that five hundred, I won it. Get it?'

I do get it. To me this adds up. I congratulate the winner, we're all in high spirits. Erich takes us to the Café de Paris. Once it's won, let it run, he says, and orders a bottle of Heidsieck Monopole. At one point you try to excuse yourself discreetly, but Erich runs after you and presses a franc into your hand. 'You're my guest tonight—if you need to piss, it's on my tab. It's on me, you hear? Everything counts at the casino.'

The bartender is attentive; Erich acts like Croesus. Everyone congratulates him.

'The secret,' says Erich grandly, 'the secret is knowing when to stop. But you need strength of character.'

We dance. Erich flirts with every pretty young woman in the room. The pastel-clad American is forgotten. You I love, Erich: you lively little marmoset, soft and good-hearted. Like a conjurer, you've magically produced this party out of thin air. You've laughed away money, you've put it in its proper place. You've played so carelessly with winning and losing, with the white and black ball, that black and white blur into one another before our eyes until we can't tell them apart anymore. You've transcended the law of gravity bestowed upon money, and magically lifted us all up with you into your fictional realm. You dance with abandon like a sylvan faun, and so may the dryads and forest nymphs appear to you and give you what you want—fleeting joy in a carefree hour.

Dearest Beloved,

I must go. As I write this I'm filled with doubts, filled with tenderness, and I can't stop crying. I've said goodbye to your bedroom, and to the mosquito net, our nightly tent. Last night I watched you sleeping there. You were beautiful, like Adam before the fall. I love you. I have to leave you and I can't leave you. I don't want to see you again, yet I long to cling to your image with my whole soul.

My love—we don't belong together. I made a mistake. I repeat this to myself a thousand times but it's no comfort. I kiss you again and again, I'm still hungry, but fourteen days from now I won't be any more satisfied. I can't see you again with your fingers green from the felt on the game-tables. Your world is not my world, your home is not my home, your happiness not my happiness, your life not my life. But it tears my heart in two. I accepted you blindly, as lover, as guide, as companion. I made a mistake. Now I'm alone again.

My love—you don't need comfort. You'll go to the Blonde, or to some other woman, you'll speed the hours till death on your par force hunt through this short life. We both know that it's short—but you want to hunt it, while I want to tend it.

Maybe you'll say, what a pity, or how stupid, or thank God. I really don't know.

I went to the market once more early this morning and bought flowers, so you won't be completely alone when you get back. Now it looks like a wedding, or a funeral. The pink carnations remind me of the Blonde. So you see, I'm not petty or jealous after all.

One last embrace; I wish you only the best. A kiss between these tears. I must go, I must go, I must go.

That's what I've written. I plan to leave it lying on your desk where it can wait for you. I take a last look around. The room is tidy. The flowers will greet you smiling. Crystal and silver gleam confidently. Your evening wear is draped over the arm-chair, immaculate and ready. This room isn't made for scenes or tears. I take my letter, my despair, my real feelings, and I rip them into tiny pieces. It's such pleasure to tear something up. I throw the pieces out the window and they catch in the palms or come to rest on the carpeting below.

For you I'll have to write something else, something completely different. Proud and even light-hearted. The way one might give a low score to a bad lover, I feel dizzy and wretched. I have a headache as though I've been drugged. But I pull myself together and start over, brief and cool. You don't care for big words.

Dear Friend:

I hoped for a cottage, a meadow, a loving animal—since children are not an option for three months or five weeks. I wanted a bit of sun and moon for us both, trees and fresh air. You wanted a hotel, every comfort, dancing at the bar in the evening. I want to live, and you want amusement. No my dear, not with me.

Adieu—I wish you the best.

That's more your line—it won't make you smile. You can easily show it to your next girlfriend, the way you like to do. It's also the truth, though only the tiniest corner of the truth. The other version is better kept to myself.

Now it's time. My God, yes—otherwise you'll be back and I'll have to talk and fight or else torture myself again at your side for another day and night.

The valet comes to help me. He gathers up my bags. I go through my room methodically, as one does when leaving a place for good, scanning one last time for the things that have been forgotten. Here is where you sat on the bed and shaved. We were happy for a short while. I've forgotten to pack my slippers. They're new, acquired just for this trip. I don't need them now, I can leave them behind: blue and lined with white, an empty sheath, a brief joy.

Then I leave quickly, wanting to put this behind me. I want to leave the hotel behind, the view of the blue sea and the too-bright sky, too carefree, teasing with its tropical glow, promising pleasure in life and joy in love, an orgy of sweet nothings. A background for love with a premature ending.

The train shudders. The panes rattle. Have I done the right thing? Or do I simply not love you enough? The recollection of last night returns, like the aftertaste of a bad meal. We sit packed tightly together around a tiny table in a small bar. Besides the Blonde, you've scared up a few new faces. Two black musicians play. The bar is so loud one has to hack through it by shouting, one's voice like an ax. The air is thick, full of sweat and smoke. To me we seem like livestock on a truck, and everyone around is full of joy, they clamor with joy at not being alone. The hostile night, the hostile starry sky, everything that lies above and beyond them is drowned out by noise and light. Elderly women dance with elderly boys, all parties appallingly smeared in make-up. You are madly amused by it all. The clock strikes two, then three, I'm half unconscious, senseless with fatigue, it simply has to end at some point, at some point this human bunch of grapes has to pull itself apart. But it only contracts more tightly. The party's still going here! call the new arrivals, plunging into our tightly packed shoebox. Room is made for them, obligingly. More people—the closeness amplifies the general pleasure. More people—it brings safety, a wall, a thicker vapor guarding against any consciousness of how senseless it is. Each person is protected from self-knowledge, it's like their own nirvana, their disintegration, and that's how they fend off their fear. Yes, I see it plainly, they have to exhaust themselves, have to spend themselves like this, down to the last degree into a stupor so they're not filled with the horror of going home, of the hotel room, the bed, the dresser mirror.

No—that's no background for love. I've done the right thing. But it's no comfort.

Now I'm headed toward Nice. I want to leave France behind—by the quickest route possible. My head drops to one side, and I fall asleep as it grows dark outside the window and the train lurches to a stop at Nice station.

'Where did *you* come from?' I ask Erich, whose little monkey face materializes before me, much to my astonishment.

Erich tells me he boarded at Beaulieu and has been observing my sleep since then; just something he likes to do. He himself is headed to Marseilles. He learns from me that I've been called back home. He pretends to believe this. Then he ponders. And he tells me I should grab my bags and disembark, at once.

'At least you should take the scenic route, dear woman! Go by Marseilles and take the bus. Go during daylight. If you don't, you'll be doing this gorgeous country a terrible injustice.'

He finds a scrap of paper and writes out the names of several towns: Saint-Raphaël and Toulon, Le Lavandou you can't miss, he grows enthusiastic, makes me eager as well, the train is still standing. Erich takes my overnight bag and tosses it to a porter, calls the name of a hotel, that will do nicely for you, yes, and he sweeps me up, hustles me out, hands me over to the porter, kisses my hand, calls out something like *enjoy yourself* and *till we meet again*, the train gives a jerk, *let yourself be tempted*, he yells after me rather enigmatically and blows me a jaunty kiss. Now the train begins to move, and I'm standing alone on a train platform as evening falls in a strange town. Doing as a man I hardly know has told me to do, I purchase a seat on the bus to Toulon. It leaves the next morning.

The bus the next morning is overcrowded. I'm not happy about the interference of well-meaning strangers. I don't know why I went along with this plan, I hate the boring coastal road we're winding down. There's nothing interesting to look at; we pass through a banal provincial resort town. Why did I spend a sleepless night in a hotel, why waste my time and money? Now the lurching bus starts to make me nauseous. And it's hot. I think of the lovely cool breeze in your car, of the comfortable, ample space beside you, of the happy looks you'd give me. The man beside me has a handlebar mustache like a harbor seal, and yesterday he surely ate garlic, and we're still hours from Toulon. It's purgatory, atonement I suppose, the road to Canossa. I wanted to let myself have a little fun, to commit a little sinful anachronism, but I can't outrun my misery, it's caught up with me here, between Saint-Raphaël and Toulon; out of the common maze of abjection I've blundered into a dead end of my own private pain.

The bus leans sharply into the curves, a sign reads 'Saint-Tropez 5 km'. A Saint Tropez, was there? Peculiar—and does this mean children here must be named Tropez, too? I'm responsible for myself now, I pull myself together: this is a geography lesson, you'll need to have stories to tell once you're home, you'll need to play up this Saint Tropez, this Saint Maxime, Canossa is no one else's business.

I can see on the map that Saint-Tropez lies on a peninsula, and that the road we're now hurtling down—in very poor shape—is a dead end. The red line runs straight for some way, then stops abruptly. We drive by grapevines and grassy meadows, several ugly villas, several neat houses, then there's a factory, it seems an unpleasant enough spot, the approach is not promising—then the bus takes a curve, for just a moment the vista opens, an image flashes up, the contoured line of a jetty ascending from the sea rounds out and blends into the warm colors of the houses, rooftops and steeples, a cheerful glimpse of the south—immediately cut off, as though this earthly perfection had materialized out of the otherworldly blue of the water just long enough to be reflected in the midday sun. But there it is again at the next turn of the road. *Le port!* someone calls out, the harbor, the harbor of Saint-Tropez. We wind down a narrow street; the magical scene now lies within reach before us, graspable yet unreal, bright and warm and glowing. Warm, yes, and gorgeously curved like an arm sweeping out before you, and not too big, just what I've been wanting. The agitated water splashes up at the jetty's edge, and in the harbor I see all the boats with their sails raised to greet me. Improbable though it seems now, it must have rained overnight. I see red sails too, vermilion defiant against the sky, boats with powerful bodies in green, ultramarine and brown, barrels being unloaded, everything alive and dancing with light and music. It's the south at midday, even the stone is friendly and radiates warmth, the strong smell of tar and fish, and I decide to stop here awhile, to explore this place, to pass through the stone arch that stands invitingly open, to sit at the Café de Paris and to stay at the Hotel Sube, whose modest façade looks out over the bright harbor.

This is love, I think—love at first sight, love already at the first half-glimpse of the harbor's bend stretching into the sea, love for each singular detail, the colorful window shutters, the warm whitewashed buildings, the touchingly small lighthouse at the end of the jetty; only love can revive as I am revived now. Yes, and suddenly I'm hungry too—all my vital spirits awakened, I'm enchanted, in a state of bliss, a heavy burden is lifted, a great emptiness is filled; the clock strikes again and the curse is broken, all thanks to love. I'm in love with Saint-Tropez.

I'm determined to stay. Not, however, in the hotel. The noise of the harbor begins at daybreak and penetrates the closed blinds in this neat, old-fashioned room with its flower-patterned carpets, fireplace and obligatory double bed. Anyway, what I want is a cottage in a meadow, now more than ever it's what I want, now that I can satisfy my own desires. Things are a bit complicated for me, here in foreign territory; I study the map, but my talent for topography was never strong; faced with this peninsula, it falls utterly flat. It's impossible for me to absorb all its inlets and promontories.

So I go to breakfast instead. This is the best decision I could have made. I eat heartily, as before a long journey, and with heart pounding I set off at last on my voyage of discovery. I try to stay close to the sea, and far from the major thoroughfare. Behind the main square planted with tall plane trees—where locals were playing boules the night before—the road begins to slope gently up. Underneath the intense blue of a cloudless sky, a sunlit ocher wall cut across at a slant by a palm has the look of African scenery. I ask myself where this road is supposed to be taking me, tell myself it's futile, this running around back roads with no signs, but I do it anyway, expectantly, even optimistically.

A two-wheeled donkey cart clatters up behind me. A farmer in a straw hat is perched on a wobbly plank, talking to his small donkey. *Espèce d'imbécile*, he says to her. Here's someone local who already knows where he's headed, I think enviously, while I'm just eating dust. Again he yells at her, *Jolie espèce d'imbécile*, hauls on the reins and the trusty cart comes to a halt; the farmer turns a friendly look my way and, with his white stubbly beard and his ancient, sweat-stained straw hat, invites me up; the little donkey can easily pull me too, it's no trouble, she's very strong, he offers proudly, well nourished, small but powerful. He reaches out a hand, pulls me up onto the plank, and now I'm enthroned on the donkey cart with him and the donkey has to prove her mettle. She races over potholes, jerking our heads violently, we jolt up and drop rudely back to earth, smile at each other, and then he asks me where I want to go and I gesture vaguely. To the right and left houses lie scattered over rolling wine country. I size them up but sadly they are all villas or farmhouses, much too big, hideous things really, with gables and turrets and unnecessary balconies. I would dearly love to ask my neighbor for his advice, but he can't understand me, the hard wooden cartwheels toss the little vehicle around and prevent all conversation. The old man stops suddenly with a lurch; he signals to me that we have reached his farmyard and asks whether I have much further to go. I climb down with effort and say goodbye to him and his donkey, he waves to me once more and turns down the narrow driveway that leads to his house. Alone again, I stand and assess my surroundings; to my left is a garden with oleander bushes through which the sea gleams, to my right runs a ditch with a dense wall of reeds concealing whatever's beyond it. There's nothing to do but keep going, see what's behind the reeds, keep hunting for a cottage just small enough for one.

And lo, there it is: behind the wall of reeds, just a few steps further, the farmer has set me down at my very door: fifty meters back from the road, among the vine rows, painted bright yellow with green shutters; the drive leads along the reed patch like a tiny ancient forest, yes, there it is: rectangular with two chimneys and a red-tiled roof, without a doubt exactly big— and small—enough. This house must be for me, I'm sure of it. God owes me this.

Across the drive stands an ox, a gorgeous dark muscled beast with gentle eyes, and in the vine rows a man and woman are working. I look closely at them: he wears a straw hat like my cart companion and a handkerchief round his neck to protect from the sun; she too wears a scarf, draped in the fashion of a nun, under a wide-brimmed hat. They appear kind, I decide, almost as kind as my gallant squire of the donkey cart. I greet them and smile, always the best prelude to conversation, and then I ask them nervously whether the house belongs to them and if it's for rent. The man and woman exchange a look, both shaking their heads, they've never rented the cottage before; they plan to move in themselves, once they're too old to work. I ask if perhaps I might have a look, just a look, and they think this over, deliberate the way farmers tend to be, and my eyes tear up in disappointment and I keep repeating *regarder*—just a look—*un coup d'oeil*, a quick look around—until the man pulls the key from his pocket with a sigh, gives it to his wife and walks like some gentle creature through the vine rows, the chemical spray at his back, stooped and patient. The woman has a good, wise face. Women are quicker. Maybe I'll win my case now that I have her to myself. We walk along the path by the reeds; she is dignified in her black costume, and I wonder how on earth I can persuade her. Nothing comes to mind. Meanwhile the cottage approaches, the entrance is at the back, she explains, we turn the corner, Oh! I say and stop still: a Grimms' fairy tale in Saint-Tropez, 'The Virgin at the Spring' on the 43rd parallel, it's much, much lovelier even than the side facing the road, it's almost like a dream. Geraniums sprout from huge clay Provençal urns, to the left of the door is an enormous marguerite daisy bush, like a huge white globe, climbing roses trim the wall, and the woman points proudly to the lemon tree which shades one window with dark-green foliage. In front of the entrance to the house, here in the middle of the vineyard, you come upon a recessed lawn, and on the lawn you see a well, and on the well's edge sit two earthenware basins, one on the right, one on the left. The woman praises the water, it's the best in the area, and as proof she lowers the bucket—Rosa von Tannenburg, I think rapturously, and look down the stone shaft with anticipation—it rises again, clear and cool and immediate, water that has never been near a pipe. I take a gulp, gush with compliments, the old woman is pleased and opens the door. We enter first into a narrow hallway, it's nice and cool here I think, wonderfully cool, and then we're in the main room, and there my delight stops short: this room, with its salmon-colored brick hearth, its walls painted pink, the floor done in red tiles, this beautiful, giant, perfectly proportioned room—is empty, absolutely empty.

I look dumbly at the old woman for a moment and ask: 'Not furnished?'

She shakes her head.

'I'd like to rent it,' I say rashly. 'You won't be needing it just yet. Do you think someone would lend me a bed?'

Bed linens, I think hopelessly, tableware, towels, oh God…

'We've never rented it before,' says the woman. 'But I might be able to loan you a bed. We do have one for my daughter's dowry.'

'She doesn't need it yet herself?'

'She's only fifteen.'

These wise people, it seems to me, are almost excessively prudent.

'So, you could loan me a bed…?' I ask, as brightly as I can.

She thinks hard for a moment. 'My daughter has a bureau, too.'

A bed and a bureau: surely some have set up house on less. It's madness, of course. But I risk it. I just need one more guarantee from the woman.

'I don't suppose you have a cat?' I inquire sheepishly. 'As small as possible, of course,' I add, as though that somehow makes it better.

Now the old farmer woman has to smile too, she smiles for a good while, finally she laughs aloud. She promises me a small cat, too. 'Around here, they come up like weeds,' she says. And then I ask the price. At this she grows slow and thoughtful again and needs to talk it over with her husband. Meanwhile, I'm free to look over the rest of the house.

The rest of the house is the kitchen. It's larger than most modern kitchens and there's an enormous fireplace, which is where I'll have to cook since there's no stove. I regard it uncertainly. But there's also a gorgeous red-tile sink and in the corner a built-in cupboard. It doesn't matter that it's not terribly elegant, that it's made of the two discarded halves of a door, it also doesn't matter that it won't close or that a spider and several unfortunate earwigs are crawling around inside. It's still a third piece of furniture. The fourth is an old table, and once I tack down a piece of oilcloth it will be like new, and the fact that it wobbles isn't really important, not for a kitchen table at any rate.

The farmer woman is standing in the doorway and I quickly close the cupboard again. It won't do, peering into other people's cupboards, no matter how empty.

'One hundred francs,' is all the woman says, because money is a straightforward thing, farmers don't waste words. One hundred francs, I think, how much is that again, keeping accounts has always been your job: all right, sixteen marks.

I nod. I pull three hundred-franc notes from my pocket. One has to be sure. Now I can't be evicted. We shake hands. No one mentions a receipt. And then she promises me her son will bring over the bed in the afternoon, the bureau as well.

I've rented a house. They wanted sixteen marks. It has a draw well, a bed, a dresser, a cat, a small meadow, a lemon tree and a quince tree, a plane tree, hundreds upon hundreds of grape vines, and among them artichokes and shell peas are growing too. I wish I could fling my arms round your neck, I want to tell you, show you that I'm not as silly and clumsy as you think I am, I can have good luck too, a different kind from yours no doubt, not luck at the gaming tables but a dreamer's luck, you benevolent gods, benevolent and redeeming gods—I want to roll around in the grass immediately, but under the farmer woman's gaze I simply walk once more through the house looking serious, trying out an air of ownership. As I do so she says casually:

'If you like artichokes or peas—help yourself, help yourself,' with a dismissive wave of the hand, as though they were all weeds. 'In the back the cherries will be ripe soon as well, they're sour cherries I'm afraid, just help yourself.'

Now I'm headed back into town. Everything here is given out freely, houses, artichokes, cherries, I won't need to spend any money at all, and I still have nearly a thousand marks, two hundred and fifty a month is what I had planned on, seven hundred and fifty for three months, one hundred for contingencies, and one hundred for the trip home. I worked all winter, every Sunday, endless Sundays, endless winter evenings, I never went out, never went to the cinema, instead I translated three huge tomes and read edits and prepared the indexes, the subject index, indexes for names and for places, the list of illustrations, and with all that work I ransomed three months of freedom, and the result is I now have no regrets about it, absolutely none.

And now I don't want to give another thought to indexes or commentaries or footnotes, instead I want to make a list of everything I need. First I write out the things that bring me joy: a reclining chair, flower vases, lights, a bedspread, cups and saucers and a pretty teapot. And a desk, stained dark, and one of those chairs with the seat woven out of straw, to put by the window. Then the list starts to get dull and dangerously long: gas stove, pots, broom, bucket, dish towels and bedlinens and silverware, grater and frying pan—Holy Tropez!—and a butter dish, a glass for my toothbrush, and I'm sure I've forgotten half of what I need.

As a new local I see the village with fresh eyes. I'm no longer drawn in by the steep alleyways; now I'm hunting for shops, fabric and ceramic stores, I'm distracted by kitchenware, and soon I've acquired a bright striped deckchair that will look splendid on the grass; and what about this garden table, painted green? Surely I'll have all my meals outside, I think grandly, so now I've bought a garden table and forgotten the stove. But the real madness, the delicious frenzy of consumption, comes over me at a store for earthenware goods. These I can bring back home with me, these are souvenirs, I reason with myself, buying a dish for the cat, plates and cups, a jam crock, a butter dish, bowls—of course, I'd completely forgotten bowls!—salad bowls and fruit bowls, a platter and vases, glazed flower vases, miniature replicas of the huge Provençal geranium pots. I'll hire a young man with a handcart and everything can be wheeled home.

At last it's evening and I'm in bed at the hotel, I've bathed as a farewell to luxury and comfort. Packages are strewn about, on the sofa, on the mantel, on the floor, the garden table and deckchair are waiting in the entryway, all my possessions are assembled about me, a rampart against bad dreams and bad memories, and I'm richer in experience: actually, nothing comes free in Saint-Tropez. Today was dreadfully expensive and I won't be counting my money tonight. I want to sleep a long, deep, sound sleep, to pay gratitude to this exhaustion.

The next day I find myself already feeling very alone. Perhaps I'm not quite up to this move. Today, there's no young man with a handcart to be seen. The fishermen are busy and brusque. I stand at the harbor square in dismay as it dawns on me: not a soul knows you, this isn't your country, and yet you want to spend three months here with your cat and your garden table; and again it all rushes back, the feeling of security by your side, the easy, carefree feeling of leaving together for some destination you've already chosen. I played the part of a woman, but now it's time once again to make decisions, to work hard, to bring order, to put the gears actively in motion.

Yes, I have my freedom and independence back, the coiled springs I need to propel me through life on the bumpy road of bachelorhood; but I haven't had my fill of dependence and being cared for, all I've been is a transient passenger before hopping off again, and now that I'm alone I have to find my own way. It wouldn't have to be a lover, boyfriend, or spouse, a father would do as well, like that one there, I think, enviously watching a pair that have just stepped off a sailboat. You've got it good, I think, I wouldn't mind having a father like that—a father with such brown skin, such white hair, such radiant eyes, with the face of a handsome sailor. Pretty blonde girl: I hope you know enough to cherish the arm he puts around you protectively and tenderly; I hope you appreciate the weathered patina on the proud figurehead at your side, magnificent wide red trousers flapping about in the wind like a pirate flag. Now one of the fishermen greets him and he waves back sociably, inimitably, raising his hand in a gesture at once informal and regal. He seems quite perfect to me, he fits into this harbor like a farmer in his field, and his blonde daughter is his match, she is tanned to the same healthy brown as he, she wears silver rings round her throat and arms like a slave, she's rather voluptuous; maybe it's a pirate ship, and the girl the human spoils of war, at peace with her fate.

The mistral blows in and I have to keep moving. The mistral is no gentle cloud chaser: it tears clothes off bodies and curtains off their rods, now the whole harbor is thrown into turmoil, the water dances, puckers in ripples, turns somersaults, is flecked with white, exuberant and frolicsome; the sky is much bluer than yesterday, the distant mountain range looks close enough to touch. It's a giddy wind, not a wind for the faint of heart, it makes you uneasy, it makes your blood thrill and your head ache, it brings drunkenness and hangover at the same time. I make a dash for the cool protection of the stone building which houses the fish market. Today I'm going to try out the frying pan and the gas cooker, I want to have a picnic at the cottage, then at three the cat arrives and the big round-the-clock cleaning begins.

At the market langoustines crawl over each other frantically in giant baskets, huge red fish like Chinese dragons gape indignantly, others are piled among them, slimy and nauseating. I can't look—mottled snake-like shapes and a pair of great plump

flat white fish with faces but no heads; I certainly won't be able
to manage those. The silver mountains of sardines alone seem
plausible. There's hardly anyone here, no other outsiders, I realize with some satisfaction. Next to me stands a young fisherman;
he looks attractive, his blue canvas trousers amply patched with
darker fabric, he has a dark tan and the look of a sailor, with
powerful shoulders and surprisingly narrow hips, and he moves
deliberately as people who work on the sea always do. I wonder
to myself if he belongs to a cargo steamer or if he's a local, until
he says, I can't believe it, he says to the fishwife, 'No no, my good
woman, that can't be right,' but he says this in German, with the
barely perceptible hint of a Berlin accent. I laugh involuntarily
and he turns to me with an especially sweet, open-hearted face,
the face of a worldly but still innocent child, so I say: 'Does the
fishwife understand German?' and he laughs and says, 'No one
here understands my French, it's too polished.' We shake hands
and I take the opportunity to ask him for fish-purchasing advice.
After a while we end up at the café, I pour my heart out to him,
he nods and listens patiently. And when I've told him everything
he stretches his shoulders till they crack, saying. 'We'll sort it all
out before long.' With a hand gesture that looks suspiciously like
he might have learnt it from the pirate, he waves a small cham-
pagne bottle and a taxi appears. 'Wait a minute,' I say, 'they have
taxis here? The idea never even occurred to me.' It turns out
there's always a line of at least three waiting right in front of the
hotel, and that I have walked by them six times a day, but never
noticed them for the simple reason that I couldn't imagine such
a thing as a taxi in this place. I still can't quite wrap my head

around it. The brown-skinned man has meanwhile picked up the garden table, he holds it on his shoulder as though it were a walking stick, whistling, and when I inquire if it isn't too heavy he only says, 'I worked as a packer in America, it's pretty good exercise,' and hoists the table easily on top of the car.

And when the car is packed full, he swings himself up on the running board because there's nowhere else he can fit, gives the driver directions, unloads everything back at the house, unwraps it, fetches water from the well, and we both begin scrubbing side by side as though we had been cleaning houses together our whole lives.

'Wolf,' I say during lunch—he's sautéed the fish to perfection, only sadly I forgot the salt—'what's your last name, anyway?'

'What does it matter?' says Wolf. 'You're not writing me any letters.'

And then while we drink coffee Wolf tells me a thing or two about Saint-Tropez. And about the figurehead I saw; the blonde girl is definitely not his daughter, 'God forbid, my dear, that would be incest,' so that clears things up. 'But don't let's get ahead of ourselves,' he adds. 'You'll see for yourself.'

And now it seems I've only seen the half of Saint-Tropez, like someone who crosses an ocean without the first idea of the flora and fauna, the octopus and sea urchins, starfish and shore crabs, this teeming underworld. I'll have to dive in, go deep into the bewildering throng of lunatics and half-lunatics that have settled around the harbor boats and behind the colored window shutters. Wolf agrees to be my underwater guide.

'You know,' Wolf says, 'I just think all the people here are so delightful. Some are a bit ordinary, of course, some are good and queer, others stay drunk all day long, but in the end everyone's really pretty funny. Now I know a girl, you've got to meet her, gorgeous, she's got curves in front and curves at the back and she's not shy about showing it off, if you know what I mean, a real redhead, so this girl, she brought a naval maneuver to a complete halt. They were meant to ship out at five in the morning and it just didn't happen. The flagship couldn't go anywhere: she was still on board, asleep. *That's* the kind of girl I'm talking about.'

He pronounces the last phrase with heartfelt appreciation.

'What about you,' I ask, 'what's your story?'

'I'm studying painting.' That's all I learn about him today because at this point the cat is delivered. She's just a little gray ball of fur, terribly small and soft with big wild eyes; I'd have liked to put her straight into my blouse and keep her there but decide that won't do while I have a male guest. Her heart beats like crazy, she scratches, struggles, hisses; the farmer's son explains to us this is her first time away from her mother. I put milk down for her in her beautiful new dish, which I did not forget, and she laps it up with her long, sleek tongue. The baby has a mustache, too. Wolf hopes it's a girl cat, not a tom. 'A dog should be male not female, but a cat the other way round,' he declares. After her meal the little one makes her bed on a wool sweater in the kitchen; we see she has a snow-white belly and white stockings on her hind paws, while on her forepaws she has only low socks. Then Wolf and I get back to work.

By evening everything is unspeakably clean. No more spiders or earwigs, and Wolf has killed a cockroach and left it on the doorstep as a warning. On the kitchen mantel sit the pretty plates and bowls, the bed is resplendent, spread with a lovely flowered cloth, inviting, cheerful and colorful; it looks like an oriental couch. Against the other wall stands the dresser, the deckchair fills one corner by the fireplace, then there's just the chimney, and that's it.

Wolf looks around, taking stock; he maintains that an empty room is always preferable to a full one, and promises to loan me two watercolors. Too bad you can't sit on a watercolor, but oh well. I desperately need a desk and chair still, and Wolf promises we'll go buy these together tomorrow; we make a date to do this at ten in the morning down by the harbor.

And then he's off. I give his hand a squeeze and he says, 'Goodbye, kid'—he was in America after all—and then he says, 'I'm a member of the Committee for the Protection of Young German Women Abroad. No special thanks from you, my good lady. You might say I've taken it on as a voluntary duty.' And with that he ambles off down the reed-lined driveway, whistling, with his rolling sailor's gait, and I'm left alone once again, in my garden, at my house. At sunset all the colors turn on once more, as though someone stepped on a switch and they lit up, swollen to a magical, supernatural sheen. This must be what the world looks like after a miracle. The dark green of the lemon tree deepens, the gold and pink of the cottage and neighboring farmhouse glow brighter and more ardently, the furrows between the vine rows intensify from earth-brown to brick-red, even my arms reflect the light as it fades and ignites at the same time, going a deep, healthy pink-brown; the sky grows still more translucent, the suspense is almost unbearable and then out of the deep silence the first birds can be heard. I've done the right thing. And it is a comfort.

The candles on the mantel are lit, uneasy and flickering. The mistral hurls itself against the shutters, clatters and howls in the chimney, wrenches at the door. I feel alone, miserable, besieged. The light isn't bright enough, it only casts shadows, yet I can't muster the will to put out the candles. I went to bed bone-tired imagining I'd have a long, healthy, country sleep, rise early, wash at the well, go for a swim in the ocean. But I reckoned without the wind, without the alien surroundings, the solitude. In daylight everything seemed glorious and peaceful, but now the reeds are rustling, the lemon tree branches are tapping eerily against the windowpanes, a dog howls, and I know: there's not a soul nearby, even the road is far away. Just one more thing for me to learn, sleeping alone at night. No shared wall, no comforting cough in the next room, no reassuring steps overhead, no people in streetcars, no grumble of a car motor driving by, no sociable greeting drawing me into a communal 'we'. I lie with eyes wide open, ears alert, in a bed that won't get warm because it's much too big for one.

It occurs to me that the kitten, across the hall in the kitchen, may be feeling as alone and afraid as I am. I badly want to fetch her, to hold something in the crook of my arm, to comfort someone else as a way of comforting myself. But how am

I supposed to get there? How am I going to make up my mind to unlock the bedroom door, then go out into the hall with its shutterless window, then into the alien and uncanny kitchen where the mouth of the fireplace yawns; how do I persuade myself to leave behind this bed, the one island in this great space, where I lie paralyzed, ears intent on catching any threatening sound. Why didn't I bring the poor creature in with me? So what if she probably isn't housebroken yet? She's adorable, warm, soft, small, maybe she'll start to purr, maybe she'll curl up around my neck. This thought, this very possibility, brings courage. I stand, take the candle from the mantelpiece, my shadow falls gigantic and distorted across the wall, but I barely look at it, I don't want to look, I don't want to be frightened; the key turns in the lock, the narrow hallway extends before me, on my right the night looks in through the window, there's the gaping mouth of the hearth in the kitchen, dark and threatening, the wind howls and whistles, and there's the wool sweater where the kitten went to sleep, the dish of milk next to it. The kitchen window—but I had closed it?—slams open, a gust of wind almost extinguishes the candle. Shivering, I close the window again, go down on hands and knees, hunt, call, cajole, rummage, my fear forgotten, all around the fireplace, every corner, even the cupboard, shine my light around the passageway, but the animal is gone, vanished, she's deserted me, she's fled somewhere out into the vineyard or the reed forest.

By now I've forgotten all my foolish, empty fears. I'm consumed instead with worry for this small creature. I had imagined it as a toy, a trinket, a piece of furniture. I acquired it just as I did the pretty glazed clay pots, never imagining it had its own fears, its homesickness; it was wild and disturbed, now it's run off and lost its way in a world it's still too small for. I tear open the front door, stand in the dark in my nightshirt and call, plead, mew, until at last from somewhere comes a thin, pitiful answer, a small, terrified sound. But I can't hear anything more beyond this answer. Finally I give up, I'm near-dead with fatigue, I sink into bed, pursued even in sleep by the kitten's plaintive mewing—it's a hot, feverish sleep and I awaken from bad dreams around noon half strangled in my sheets.

Getting up is always a chore. I ignore the fact that no one has ever died of getting up in the morning. Not from getting up, from washing, from brushing teeth. The sun shines through the window: it's terribly late.

One has to enjoy the advantages of solitude. I walk naked and carefree out the door and into the yard. This lasts no more than a second. '*Charmant, charmant,*' Wolf says; he's set up his easel immediately in front of my door.

I swear, quickly throw on my bathing suit, then come back out and swear some more. I deliver a lecture on privacy, on being a recluse, on the desire for solitude. But Wolf just goes on painting, shrugging occasionally, and eventually he says, 'My dear, I can see you've slept very badly.' At this we both laugh, and I tell him of course I'm pleased to see him here. And he stands and pulls the chair over, isn't it an excellent find, he bought it between ten and noon when I failed to show up and he was waiting for me. And with that everything rushes back to me from yesterday, one thing above all—

'Wolf, the kitten got out.'

Wolf understands the gravity of this immediately. He leaps down into the ditch by the forest of reeds, patrols this tiny jungle, startles the lizards and finds a turtle. We mew and mew, we put on a concert like a full cat orchestra. We set out milk dishes as lures. Occasionally the poor orphan answers; even after we begin to abandon hope and Wolf clambers back out of the ditch we hear occasional cries. But we have no idea where the sound is coming from. It seems to come from here, then over there, then somewhere else again. It drives us mad. Under a different sky we might have given up much sooner. But here with this blue, this silence, among the flowers, trees, birds and butterflies, even this small cry, from this small creature, bears enormous significance: it tears the mild, clear noon so beseechingly we can't bear it.

'She's hungry,' says Wolf. So we fill still more dishes with milk, we distribute them in carefully calculated locations around the yard; hard to imagine a creature going hungry in this cottage's environs, here, so close to this peaceful roof, this draw well, this daisy bush.

Until at last we ourselves can't keep up the hunt because of our own hunger. Wolf persuades me to take a walk into town. 'We'll have to hold off until evening. Then at least her eyes will reflect light in the dark.'

We walk peacefully along the country road, like children on their way to school.

'Why are you being so kind to me?' I ask.

Wolf abruptly stops his idle whistling. He looks at me

astonished. 'Kind? What do you mean?—I mean, I really hadn't thought about it. That's just how I am.'

So that's all it is. He's always like this; don't take it personally. Always, to everyone, cats too. I chew on this awhile.

'I believe that's what's called good nature,' I say. 'But in the end there's nothing so very special about being good-natured. Lots of people are. In my opinion, it's because it's much easier to be good than to be evil. What do you think?'

Wolf doesn't notice my irritation. 'You know, I really never gave it much thought.'

'You're telling me you've never thought about it at all?'

'No, I told you, not at all. Life is too marvelous to think so hard about it. Don't you think it's marvelous? Take this tree,' he comes to a stop reverently in front of a looming umbrella pine, 'it's simply wonderful. And thinking about it doesn't make the tree something else. It just doesn't. *And now come along, kid,*' he says in English, putting his arm through mine, '*I am terribly hungry.*'

He pulls me along at his pace, and whistling and skipping we arrive in Saint-Tropez, where the harbor is full of sails flapping like flags; we end up at a little restaurant with gaily checked curtains, tablecloths and plates. Because of the hour, we'll get only whatever they have left. Wolf says it's fine by him. We sit, and then receive a gigantic platter of garlic sausages, ham, olives, pâté, sardines, anchovies, sliced tomatoes and onions and hard-boiled eggs all piled together, a copious and piquant first course, harbinger of things to come. It's much too late for the French to be eating, so we're all alone; nearby in the tiny kitchen they're washing up, flies are buzzing, it's dark, cool and quiet.

'You do look tired. Bad sleep?'

I confess I didn't sleep well. But it's more than just that. 'If I really stop and think about it, this past week felt like being shoved through a meat-grinder by some divine, inexorable hand. And it's only now that I'm starting to get my life back together, in a foggy and back-to-front way—not an uplifting feeling.'

Wolf's got a mouthful of gristly sausage, he swallows carefully, then he looks at me and says: 'You seem like you're holding on to some overwhelming pain. You've been chewing it over and over and over, you should just spit this thing out and stick it under the table.' And then he pushes his straw hat from the right to the left ear—he never takes it off, otherwise he would leave it somewhere and risk sunstroke—it looks absurd, and I have to laugh, but he looks at me again with a straight face and says emphatically: 'Life is magnificent. And so is this sausage, by the way. So eat.'

It's doing me good, infinite good, not being alone. Some guardian angel must have lined up Erich and Wolf on my path, like relay stations on a grueling journey. I really feel as if I've been saved, rescued by life itself. I smile at Wolf, who's silently devouring his sausage; a pretty waitress arrives with our first serious course, a tureen aromatic with herbs. She gives us both large portions, places them on the table proudly, and at once the whole scene disintegrates, the smiles, the safety, the first foray, the fresh confidence. I sit in front of my dish and inhale the rising scent of saffron and seafood, unbearably it transports me to another noonday meal. Enchanted, I look back into the past through the steaming bouillabaisse; like the smoke from a sacrificial fire its color and fragrance call up your voice and face, everything I've blotted out or wanted to, then they irrevocably summon still more: the bliss of proximity, of contented harmony, unmixed devotion, floating on air without so much as the beat of a wing.

Yes, here I am, a comical figure, bewildered and crying a torrent of tears into my soup plate, unashamed.

'There now, let's not over-salt such a good soup,' says Wolf. But he says it very gently, and he takes the unlucky plate from me and the tureen too, removing all evidence from the room with care. And he stays discreetly out of sight long enough for me to blow my nose and fix up my face, the clean-up after the storm.

And then we go on eating. You should always keep eating. Food has a calming power. Life will always reel you back in.

Wolf will do no such thing, however. He drags me afterward to the café. Beneath the canopy sits the handsome old pirate with his silver-braceleted slave. 'Hi!' says Wolf, before bring-ing me over to their table. The pirate is uncharacteristically forthcoming for an Englishman, he welcomes me gregariously, even treats me to coffee. We sit, a tired and lazy foursome in the sun, we make a kind of family, what ties us together is the only worthy bond: love, love of the same thing, love that can't degenerate into envy, because it is for Saint-Tropez alone.

The girl's name is Marianne and she's from Vienna. After half an hour I know her life story. How little money she has, that her mother is dead and that she's not welcome at her father's and that's why she has to travel cheaply, that she loves the old pirate ardently and jealously in spite of his missing teeth.

'You can't imagine the power of attraction he has over women.' I nod, in fact I can easily imagine it. I squeeze Marianne's hand and think: 'Under all that colorful plumage she's just like me.'

'Unfortunately he's completely unprincipled. Well, my own principles aren't all that rigid either, but I'm basically faithful. And I've thought it out clearly, you know after all he's so awfully much older than I am and he could just be happy I'm there with him. You know I'm not really as frivolous as I seem, chasing pleasure and that sort of thing, I'll take care of him when he's sick, anyway I'd certainly never leave him. When I arrived here he was so lonely, and the state of things on his boat, you should have seen it, and then I came along and tidied up, the first thing I did, I cleaned for three days. At the beginning we were madly happy, so happy everyone said they couldn't even look at us, so much happiness wasn't natural.'

'Even when I saw you yesterday morning, you were positively radiant.'

'Yes, but these days that's all temporary. He gets more difficult by the hour. And as far as *my* emotional needs, he's not the least bit interested anymore. When I bring up the future he just laughs. Then he thinks all the other girls are pretty and plays the flirt with them, even if I'm there, and when I get angry—you have to have some pride, after all, don't you think?—then he laughs. He takes feelings so lightly, and I actually have to explain to him, hey, I'm not just here for you to sleep with. That's nice too of course and it's part of the deal, I've got nothing against it at all, on the contrary; but when I've spent the whole evening mad at him and in the end all he says to me is come to bed you stupid girl—well, then I'm not really in the mood. Then we fight, and he really doesn't take in a word I'm saying, he simply doesn't give me anything back. It's that German sentimentality, that's what he always says, you shouldn't take everything so seriously. But you see he's such a handsome man—so much more attractive than most of these younger men, he knows everyone, he's had such an exciting life and been everywhere, he's been to the South Seas and he introduced me to Chaplin. He really is terrific, even if he does have no money and only chose this place to dock his boat because there's no harbor fee. But unfortunately he can manage perfectly well without me, because all the women are crazy about him. And the worst part is, there's no talking it through with him. If you sit down and talk it out, things are always easier. But he doesn't want to hear it, just wants to have fun and enjoy life, and he's always telling me I'm a spoilsport.'

Meanwhile the old gray pirate has been chatting animatedly with Wolf. Now he winks at me, in high spirits. He reaches across the table and pats Marianne's hand, as though soothing a dog.

'Telling tales about me again, is she? But don't you go believing everything she says'—he switches in and out of English—'*she is a stupid little girl*. Really, a stupid little girl. A scene is what she wants—yes, a scene, and she wants it with me.' He roars with laughter and turns to me. 'She gets furious if I don't listen to her. I'm an old man'—here he's coy—'and we old fellows need our peace. Just don't get worked up, I say; I never do. *What a sweet little girl*,' he suddenly says. 'See her?' And he waves at a young woman passing by. His eyes are surprisingly good for an old man's. '*Charming*.' Then he gestures with his thumb at his girlfriend. 'She always has to make love into a problem. Not with me, my girl. I got this old without any problems. *Not really old, you know*.' He puffs out his powerful chest and strikes it with satisfaction. 'Live and let live, that's my way. *Don't bother*. And that's good enough for me. Everything else is bunk. And if it doesn't suit you, my girl, *you can go back to your Einstein*. But you're not smart enough for him. She's not so bright, if you really want to know. Only imbeciles think they have to make life complicated. *You are a fool, that's what you are*.'

Marianne has tears in her eyes. The pirate is suddenly furious. He can see blood, but not tears. So it is, with so many men. 'There, look at her, cry over nothing all you want, there she goes again. Cry at three, cry at four in the afternoon. Get back to the boat, you stupid thing.' With a gesture of command he banishes her from the table and she leaves, like a concubine who's fallen from favor. I cautiously suggest he could treat her a bit more kindly. 'Tears should be a compliment to any man. They always come from the heart.'

'She makes me look like a fool,' he says, 'but I'll show her. I'm the most patient person in the world, *really*, a friend to everyone, but I'll never let a mood spoil my fun. If she doesn't like it, she can keep moving. Plenty of other lovely girls, the world's full of them, let her think about that. Instead of making faces and crying her eyes out and sitting around like three days of rain.' With that the pirate pays angrily, nods, and is gone.

'Will he beat her?' I ask Wolf.

'The fellow's much too lazy for that.'

We sit awhile under the umbrella, there's a man in the café who's been drinking himself to death for years with whiskey, he'll never get away, explains Wolf, because he simply can't make it to the bus anymore, one day he'll just keel over dead off his barstool. One less crazy person; it hardly matters.

Women pass by us dressed up in the local uniform: linen pants, brick-red or blue, and on top a kerchief tied in a triangle over the bosom, always fastened to a necklace. Sometimes it looks good, sometimes grotesque, depending on what's underneath.

'Got any money?' asks Wolf, out of nowhere.

'How much?'

'Twenty or thirty marks.'

'What for?'

'I can't let you run around here one more day looking like you do. You're a disgrace to Tropez, to the whole region.'

I'm wearing a very pretty pale summer dress and a very pretty white straw hat with a blue band, which the Blonde picked out and you paid for.

'You're wearing a skirt,' says Wolf in disgust. 'Trousers, it's got to be trousers, you'll feel like a new person. Come on.'

He bundles me into a tiny shop overflowing with motley kerchiefs, caps, sandals, shorts, pants, huge bales of dyed cotton. An unfriendly heavy-set woman keeps guard like a watchdog.

'This lady would like to go Tropézienne,' Wolf tells her.

She looks me over with a scowl, like a sculptor squinting at a badly cut block of marble which she now has to make into a monument. She doesn't ask what I want. She puts me in rust-red capri pants; to my demurral, I don't wear red and I don't want to wear red, she only says, 'You don't know the first thing about it.' On top of the red pants she adds a blue shirt, not a pale blue and not a dark blue but a bold royal blue, throws a hat on top a meter in diameter, rips it off again, puts on another, never once asks my opinion, barely lets me look in the mirror, never mentions a price, storms around tyrannically, brooks no contradiction. In the end she looks me over, still not content, as if to say you try to do something with this material, spins me around for Wolf to see, and as my eye falls on the mirror, blaring red and blue, Wolf enthusiastically approves.

'I look like—' I pause. 'Like—'

'Like a Van Gogh. Now pay.'

So I do. Wolf won't stand for rebellion either. The shop is at least reasonable. The hat costs two marks fifty. Some comfort.

'Fantastic,' says Wolf. 'It looks fantastic on you. Then again when one's as slim as you are—'

Even the broken-hearted don't mind hearing that sort of thing. Wolf always speaks with total conviction.

It's the kind of outfit you get used to quickly, it boosts confidence and helps overcome hang-ups. It's easy to feel light and sure in hemp-soled espadrilles. I put my hands in my pockets; let the mistral blow in again, nothing can sweep up my skirt now. I get the urge to run, do cartwheels, my limbs want to test their new freedom.

'You're going to be just fine here,' says Wolf. 'But it takes time to realize it. The old guy has it exactly right, actually. You have to take life as it comes. Now, I used to be a bit of a drag myself. I used to overthink things—can I paint, do I have talent, do I have the right to live this way and never do anything reputable, worthy, sensible. My father, he's a salesman. By the time he was twenty-five he already had a family. No one's going to say that about me. But I don't worry about that anymore, I don't even think about it. You have to swim or you'll drown—but you can't think about drowning while you swim. Life is unpredictable and sublime. Once you understand that, you won't be afraid. Not even at night.'

We're walking home now. I'm rather in awe of Wolf's words. He suddenly comes across as terribly mature.

'You see,' says Wolf, 'I'm in love with accidents. You imagine things one way, then something else happens. It's because people think things should go just as they've imagined that they're unhappy when they don't—and then they can only fixate on how things should have gone.' We've arrived at the cottage, the reed path in front of us. 'Sure, you might have imagined and planned things differently. I haven't asked you much so far, and I won't ask. People think you always have to speak your thoughts, but I don't hold with it. That's just chewing your cud instead of finding new fodder. Right now you're here and you're here alone, and you're living in your regrets because you're not here as part of a couple. But that's nonsense. You have to keep on being new, if you see what I mean. You've brought all your old ideas with you into this new world, all the old wants and all the made-up scenes, and that's wrong. See? Now you've got the pants, you can stop worrying about yesterday's skirt. Now you can jump over the ditch yourself.'

It's true, I can. I jump over the ditch. Wolf watches me and he doesn't offer his hand.

'Let's get back to that cat,' is all he says.

The milk traps are still there, apparently undisturbed. Same with the dish of sardine oil. My heart sinks.

'We'll never get her back.'

'Why not?'

'She's too small.'

'Come on,' says Wolf. 'Let's see if she's still there.'

I mew. At this point I've had so much practice, I've practically mastered it. And there, a tiny voice answers. Now we have to find her and catch her. I walk, still mewing, I follow the sound, crouch down in front of the bushes where it's coming from, keep mewing, the answering voice keeps up with me.

'You distract her,' Wolf whispers. 'I'll come round from behind.'

She's hiding in the thicket of reeds between the ditch and the road. Wolf climbs softly, carefully into the ditch, creeps stealthily along while I mew like crazy; if our calculations are correct she should be close between us. Suddenly there's a yell—Wolf roars, 'Quick, quick, take this monster away from me!' He thrusts a wildly struggling, pedaling, thrashing something at me and I take it gingerly by the nape so that it curls up into a ball.

'That she-devil bit me,' says Wolf. 'That's the last time I hunt a predator.'

The predator is terribly skittish. A day and a night out in the open have left her in a frenzy. She trembles, bristles, darts her wide eyes around; she hisses, but she doesn't bite anymore. And the sardine oil disappears in barely a second.

Wolf mutters curses while he washes out his wounds, and I pay no attention. When the small creature begins to lap up milk with abandon, however, Wolf betrays a fatherly pride and pleasure. To me she is indescribably sweet, and once she's finished her meal I stick her in my blouse—or rather, in my shirt—where at first she thrashes around some more, but without scratching; gradually calmed by warmth and darkness, she resigns herself, at peace. She stops trembling, her pounding heart slows, now she breathes gently, in and out, in and out.

'Now I'm a third wheel,' says Wolf. 'I'll look in on the two of you tomorrow, and I'll bring a real sardine for the little one, no more of those tinned cadavers.'

We shake hands.

'Goodbye, kid,' says Wolf, 'get some sleep,' and he's gone. The truth in a word is I love him. But differently; so very differently.

In the evening I come back out into the yard. My small companion has escaped from me again and withdrawn to the furthest corner under the bed, still a tiny bundle of homesick misery. It's going to take time to tame her, but I don't want anything more for free, in fact I think it's beautiful that it should be so difficult to bring even such a small animal out into the world. Gradually she'll be transformed, just as children learn to walk and talk only gradually; it takes lots of time and lots of patience.

The moon is out as well this evening, a moon completely bright, and I'm not frightened of shadows anymore. The lemon and small plane tree are motionless, the reed patch too stands still as a wall. I sit on the edge of the well and look around at my small world; the moonlight suits the daisy bush nicely, it's as white as it is in daylight. Wolf is right, I think. Life is magnificent, as soon as you can be content with it. Anything else is false. To yield, just as you take the water trustingly into your arms when swimming; if you have no fear, then you can't go under. Fear is the only false thing. To be always on high alert, that's false. To indulge in sinister thoughts is false. The thing to do is to put yourself in the arms of life. Just as they used to give in to God's command. Maybe, after all, it's not so different.

The calendar tells me it's the 15th. I almost don't believe it. It's been fourteen days since I arrived here—*fourteen days*. They reach back behind me like a long chapter of life, lazy hours lying in the sun on the grass, swallows diving over me, tracing with my eyes the graceful curves of the terracotta roof tiles. Evening falls more and more slowly. Endless beach hours, endless hours being rocked on the water. Only here and there a brief intermission on land: doing dishes at the well, picking up groceries from the farmer or in the village, making the bed, the gas cooker bursting into flame. The daisy bush has gone by. Five giant sunflowers, with their regal picture-book faces, have replaced it.

It's noon. The bed is made, the kitchen is clean, the tiled floor is waxed and everything is gleaming, lunch is harvested and on the table. I've made potatoes and new peas, with artichokes in oil and vinegar to start, cherry compote for dessert. All from my own little plot of land.

I'm waiting for a guest. I have no shortage of visitors. Wolf brings fresh fish for our cat-child, and Marianne regularly needs a shoulder to cry on. She still doesn't know my own story, thank God. She takes me for an unrepentant virgin with an underdeveloped erotic life.

She arrives as I'm laying the table. Dressed in cornflower-blue with silver toenails, imagining herself a fancy Parisian prostitute. The pirate is right: she is a silly little girl. But there's nothing wrong with that.

Marianne hugs me. From her bag she pulls a small package 'just for the cat'. The cat has gradually become an attraction in her own right. She's been christened and now answers to the name Colette, in honor of the great writer whose summer house is several properties down. She really does answer to the name. Colette! I call, and she responds immediately, her voice comes down to us from somewhere high up, she loves to roam around in the trees and then at my word she appears.

Now comes Colette's hunger dance. I show her the meat and she immediately begins a pretty paso doble on her hind paws, while with her front paws she grabs beseechingly, snatching at the air, mewing all the time as though she's been starved for the last fourteen days.

'She's in a growth spurt,' I say, making excuses for her greediness. Marianne expresses approval of her beautiful smooth, silky coat, and we both observe that her tail, which at first looked like an overused toothbrush, is now approaching angora-like proportions. Once these rituals are over, we sit down to eat.

'How are you?' I ask. How are you—for us this means, what's the latest in love and rivalry.

Marianne says, between artichoke leaves, 'He's gone too far. I've done all I can for him and I've put up with everything. But there's a limit. Tell me, what should I do?'

'Walk off the boat for good,' I advise her. 'Make yourself scarce. What's he done this time?'

Apparently he's done plenty and his list of crimes is very long, but this latest, says Marianne, this latest kicks the bottom out of all the barrels in Saint-Tropez.

'You know how I manage the laundry on board. I make sure the beds are always freshly made up. And then today he says to me—' she fights back tears—'he says to me today, first thing over breakfast, and I've just made the coffee, he says: a new girl's coming, could you put down fresh sheets. Those were his words: *new girl coming, new sheets!*'

'But why, why in God's name do you let yourself be trampled over that way? Be independent! Go rent a room for yourself!'

Marianne looks at me. She's a silly girl, but a good person, and what she says next a thousand other silly good girls would say too, girls who will make coffee, darn socks and make up beds in return for a little love:

'But it's still paradise compared with the pathetic emptiness and tedium of living alone, when you can't enjoy either the advantages or drawbacks of being in a couple. Positively the worst thing of all is getting stuck alone and with no money.

'I should have gotten married,' Marianne goes on. 'But no one has any money. So you take what's on offer. And I really did love him. And when you're in love, of course, you want to be together. Nothing else makes any sense. It's easy for you to say leave him; but trust me, the most important thing of all is to live with someone.' Suddenly she bursts out again: 'What am I doing wrong, what's wrong with me that I should be treated this way? I'm not a bad person. Just naïve.'

'There's too much supply,' I say. 'In Brazil they use coffee for fuel, or just throw it in the ocean. But you can't just dump extra women in the ocean. These days men are the great prize.'

'Right,' says Marianne, 'and the idiots know it all too well. It completely spoils them. They don't have to make any effort at all. Being men is enough. They all think they're rare valuable stamps, like a three-penny Red Saxon. But at the end of the day nothing's changed, they're still worth three pennies.'

After a pause, Marianne says, 'You're looking well. I envy you. You really don't have a boyfriend?'

I answer truthfully that I have none. But Marianne means something else.

'That only works when you have nothing to compare it to. Before you've tried it, you're none the wiser. Once you've experienced it, you can't do without it so easily. I'm not the sort to deprive myself.'

I go into the kitchen to make coffee, Marianne lies outside sunning herself. The kitchen is peaceful and quiet, a world without men. I wait for the small copper coffee pot to fill three times over and avoid my thoughts.

Someone comes into the kitchen just as the third pot is coming to a boil.

'Don't you ever knock?' I say.

'I've got other things on my mind,' says Wolf, and sits down on a three-legged stool that's been banished to the kitchen. 'I'm the bearer of sad news, and to be honest, this news goes particularly against my sunny nature. There's a new slave aboard the pirate ship. That feisty old fart is having a wedding party and he's put Marianne's suitcases by the door, by which I mean the gangplank. He left them high and dry on the harbor square. That is, until I took care of them. They're safe with me for now. But someone has to tell her.'

'I don't have much practice with this kind of thing,' I say.

'In cases like these, I usually just write a letter,' says Wolf.

Meanwhile, the coffee is ready. We go out together to Marianne, who's lying in the grass oblivious and smoking.

We drink in silence. A deep quiet prevails for five more long summer minutes. Then Marianne gives a heart-rending sob, Wolf shrugs his shoulders despondently, says he's too soft for this and it's not his fault, then goes inside with Colette. From within we hear him sing 'That's the Way Sailors Love', which must be due to absentmindedness since he's usually so tactful.

Marianne cries herself dry, she cries and cries, it must feel wonderful to be able to just turn on the tap and let all your sorrows run out until all you feel is emptiness, until you feel empty and numb. And after she's spent her reserve of tears, she dumps out whole sackloads of grievances old and new in front of me, full of the past and life's disappointments. I hear all about Ferdinand and about Kurt and about why she couldn't marry Alfred, and how many men she's been madly in love with before finding out it was going nowhere.

She's drowning me, I'm up to my neck in this torrent of memories, I'd like to save myself but nothing seems to help. Marianne is purging her soul. Remorselessly. She holds nothing back. Every hotel rendezvous, every weekend away, every time she's been out late dancing, each brief radiance, each new hope. Suddenly she interrupts herself to say—

'How you must despise me now!'

But I don't, not at all. Maybe before. Now, though, I find it miraculous the way she always picks herself up again, inexhaustibly naïve, inexhaustibly gullible, somehow when the same words are uttered by someone new never anticipating the same disappointment, only the same song of love.

Thank heaven Wolf returns. Marianne has calmed herself a bit. But she looks a fright, as though a tornado or a tidal wave had crossed her face. Wolf is a diplomat. He has an idea.

'Kids,' he says, 'we're going to show that old ass. Marianne, if you agree not to be a wet blanket, we can give him back a bit of his own medicine. Then he can see what it's like to get mad, too. This guy thinks you're going to go straight to bed and chew on your pillow. He'll be full of masculine pride and he'll say, I hope that girl doesn't try to do herself in, she was crazy about me. So I say let's go have a wild night out, us three. Marianne will make us a trio. We can show the ass how long it takes to get over losing him.' Wolf claps Marianne on the shoulder. 'Chin up, chin up my girl. Tonight is the big gala at L'Escale. I'll get us a table.' Then he turns to me and says, 'It's high time you got acquainted with the local nightlife. We'll head over there at nine. First to the fishermen's ball, the pirate won't go near it, thinks he's too good. We'll start by getting soused there, and then at ten, when you're good and dizzy, we'll move on to the upscale place. Now let's pool our money.'

We pool our money, collect sixty francs for tonight—that should be enough to make it one for the books.

'We're going to make that conceited old beggar so mad he'll finally feel self-conscious about his false teeth,' says Wolf. 'Now, let's go back to my house, Marianne darling, and make you gorgeous.'

At nine on the dot I drop by Wolf's to pick up Marianne. Both are looking their best. Wolf is freshly shaven, he's wearing a new sweater and he has a part in his hair, he smells like soap and brilliantine, but that's nothing next to Marianne: all her nails are freshly painted silver, her eyebrows and lashes a deep black, her heart-shaped mouth coral-red, she has her hair newly done in curls. She must have been hard at work the whole afternoon.

'Hasn't she made a marvelous exhibit of herself?' asks Wolf. 'The only thing is, the frame ought to be just a little wider.'

The frame has indeed been reduced to the bare minimum. Arms, shoulders, back are completely naked, and what little covering there is elsewhere is practically see-through.

'She's been at it till practically this minute,' whispers Wolf. 'First the hair, then the manicure, and now that her eyes are done she can't cry anymore.'

We walk contentedly to the fishermen's ball. It's a pleasant stroll through narrow, steep streets, under the lanterns' dim light, past the over-fed cats, out to the edge of the village. For a moment we stand still; to our left the wash-house looks almost like a Christmas chapel with its pretty arcades. Despite the late hour the lights are still burning, the women inside hard at work. From the village we can hear music, the raw sounds of popular dance music: gramophone, electric piano, orchestrion. The night is electric, quite unromantic, in spite of the castle which fills in the scenic background like a painting. The sound takes over our limbs. Wolf stretches his arms till his joints crack and says: 'Now let's have some fun,' and he extracts a promise from both of us to dance with every lad at the fishermen's ball who asks us to, unless we want to insult someone. 'If you're not going to join in, don't show up. Ladies and gentlemen, this is entertainment for the people.'

The fishermen's ball happens under the trees, out in the open. A fenced-in square of concrete with a mighty orchestrion, wooden benches and tables set up here and there, and above all this a network of light bulbs. The place is packed and we're embarrassed by our trousers, since all the women are wearing dresses and the men are in their Sunday suits.

One duo I recognize, the garage mechanic and the son of my farmer couple, we nod to one another. Everyone is sitting around politely until all at once a fat man makes the machine go and the orchestrion strikes up, raucous. It only has one volume setting: ELEVEN, it hammers out its mechanical rhythm deafeningly, one after another couples find each other, children join in, and there are male pairs dancing too, acrobat-dancers, they spin each other with unbelievable speed, hats pulled rakishly askew. Only a few, not so fine, wear caps and bright kerchiefs instead of collars. I watch and it makes me giddy, the dance is done in very small mincing steps, tiny and fast. It's a brightly exuberant picture, all the girls are in light-colored silk dresses—pink, yellow, blue—the skirts billowing out like balloons, all with very serious faces, composed and intent, no one speaking. One couple is being followed around by a dog, confused and excited. Women, men and children perch on the walls of neighboring houses to watch. The dance seems endless, and when the contraption has run through its song roll the fat man cries *Attendez!* and gets ready to start the whole thing over.

Abruptly tame and civilized, the pairs then decamp from the wild animal cage through a narrow gate, and the fat man charges five sous per dance. The men pay.

The second roll blasts out at a breathtaking tempo. Wolf is in the ring with Marianne. He fits right in here, his cap tugged low over his eyes, and he dances just like the fishermen, one hand pressed to his partner's backside, with the same small, precise steps in three-quarter beats at the same frenzied speed. I'm not allowed to watch for long. Here, no girl gets to sit out a dance. There's a glut of men and no one plays the superior bystander. My partner is an excellent dancer, with a natural gift for the dance, an easy buoyancy; he spins me, twirls me, holds me lightly in his arms, smells like violet pomade and garlic. We dance the entire dance at the same relentless clip until my knees are shaking. Then he pays, polite and shy, accompanies me back to my table without a word. I wipe the sweat from my face unselfconsciously. Having fun is hard work.

Marianne is beaming. 'It's impossible not to be happy when you're this dizzy, it doesn't matter how hard you try!'

We keep this up for another hour or so. We don't sit out a dance. It's an exhilarating feeling for once to have one's pick of unlimited resources. The fresh, cool air makes us resilient. The orchestrion plays like an African war drum, repetitive and rousing. I think back with disdain to the bars and cafés in Nice and Monte Carlo. No one gets drunk here. Everything seems to come straight from nature. No moment is dead, because everyone is alive.

Wolf pulls out his watch, a great nickel-plated thing, two marks fifty he says proudly, and it always goes right.

'It's time—get a powder and a comb in, kids, so you don't disgrace me.'

'It's lucky you have two arms,' I say, and then with Wolf in the middle we walk on, entangled arm in arm, past the fishing harbor where the nets have been hung to dry, sit down for a bit on the damp stones, plunge our toes in the water lapping up at us, with an occasional shriek, and Marianne says: 'Having friends is the best thing. But a plan's a plan, and now I think it's time to go make that pirate sorry.' And suddenly she throws her arms around Wolf and says, 'I'm so grateful. And if I ever curse men again, which I'm afraid will probably be often, I'll be sure and add: except for Wolf.'

'You'll catch your death, darling,' says Wolf. We stand up again, walk through the night in this enchanted place we all love; I think how forlorn our poor Marianne would be if she were in Vienna on a rainy evening in the same state she's in now, and what a stroke of luck it was that washed the three of us up here together. I thank God fervently for Saint-Tropez, the brightly lit wash-house, these minutes spent by the old harbor, the lights on the far shore; for the warm air, the gentle sounds of the sea, the even rhythm of our steps on the Place de la Mairie.

At last we wind up at L'Escale, the most famous dance hall on the coast, where you might spot the likes of Mistinguett, Lilian Harvey, Gloria Swanson and other luminaries from the film industry's firmament. Cars are packed in between the barrels set up by the harbor, from Cannes, Saint-Raphaël, Sainte-Maxime—Rolls-Royces, LaSalles, Cadillacs, delegates from all the foremost automobile dynasties.

The interior feels like a long tube or a stretched-out box, with benches and tables along the walls and a narrow strip down the middle for dancing. There's no transparent glass floor, no elaborate light fixtures, no secluded corners. But it does have a fabulous hostess, a cross between a frog and a French bulldog, short and heavy, with watery eyes, pert turned-up nose, meaty hips and short legs stuffed into capri pants, bosom overflowing her triangular bib. We christen her the Frog Queen. She waddles up to us, extends a gracious hand, welcomes us to her realm and points us to a table. Off in a corner, with disheveled hair and a ravaged face, the Frog Queen's boyfriend is reclining sullenly. It's rumored that he hates people, and it seems to be true. Wolf believes he's enormously talented, but he seems to have contempt even for his own talent; he wastes it all on the decorations, which are destroyed when they're changed every few weeks. The beloved silhouette of the harbor greets us bewitchingly, cut from shiny paper and pasted up on the wall, with its church tower and tiled rooftops, on the other side the boats, the lighthouse and the sea. One floor up, from paper opera boxes beautifully sculpted Negro busts look down at the tumult, along with white-bearded Mussulmans and veiled women from a seraglio, everything fashioned out of paper.

This is my first time here, which is criminal for such a set-tled Tropézienne, but this is exactly what I was running away from, and you have to show some consistency. But here it's completely different from the civilized Côte d'Azur. The Frog Queen is something else, something wilder and more barbaric than your average tame barkeeper. The clientele is different. Next to me at the table sits a hefty guy, a faded newsboy cap pulled down low over the hollow where one of his eyes should be. A blue and white striped fisherman's shirt is stretched over his bulging belly. I wouldn't want to meet him in a dark alley. Across from him is a woman wearing too much make-up and a flaming-red silk dress. She shoves her legs between his knees and gazes adoringly at him. I nudge Wolf.

'Oh that,' he says. 'My dear, you innocent virgin of Saint-Tropez. You have so much to learn. Just wait till you see what happens with that man as the night goes on…'

'I could imagine him as a smuggler with a boat full of opium and alcohol. That would explain the gouged-out eye.'

'Him?' says Wolf. 'You mean to tell me you've never seen him before? Look closer at the gorilla's chest, *darling*!'

On his striped sweater it says in big letters TAM TAM. I stare at this insignia with wide eyes. Does it mean he's a member of something like the Ku Klux Klan, or is there some kind of mafia here, and this big shot is the official head of the organization, feared but tolerated? Suddenly I let out a little cry.

'He just winked at me. Wolf, oh my God, you'll protect me, won't you?'

Wolf laughs, he laughs long and uproariously. Finally he explains to me that TAM TAM is the abbreviation for 'Maritime Transport' or something like that, and that this big shot runs the shuttle between Saint-Tropez and Sainte-Maxime, back and forth all day long, harmless, no threat at all. By day, anyway, Wolf adds.

'But that's no excuse for him winking at me!'

'He thinks you're rich,' says Wolf. 'And he thought you wanted something from him.'

At this I'm even more bewildered. 'From that monster?' But Wolf nudges me as I say this, and I see a gorgeous, dainty blonde, straight out of a fairy tale, wearing a white silk confection—only a truly visionary designer could have dreamt up and then realized such a thing—and she leans close to Caliban, she lays her hand on his shoulder and before you know it the monster is dancing with the nymph, and he dances just like the men at the fishermen's ball, his big brown paws with nails missing splayed across her delicate haunch while she leans enraptured on his shoulder. It looks like a movie poster: the gorilla seduces the young bride. Except this bride seduced the gorilla.

Wolf says: 'You and I will never fathom the secrets of love. Anyway, women can't get enough of this guy; here he's chic.'

'I've always imagined a gigolo rather differently,' says Marianne. 'At least he should have a glass eye made.'

'He simply doesn't give it a thought. And that increases his charm. Women love variety. Two eyes—they've already got that themselves.'

At that moment Marianne gives me a sharp pinch on the arm. The pirate! A parlor-pirate at the moment—more elegant than ever in sulfur-yellow silk trousers, accompanied by an athletic redhead with a broad Slavic face.

'Ohhh!' says Wolf, and then, 'Marianne, you can't compete with that. This girl is a nautical specialist. She's the one I told you about, with the naval maneuver. They ought to hire her in the next war to suppress hostilities.'

The pirate looks over at us, visibly disconcerted. He gives a brusque greeting. Wolf grins. 'Come on love, let's go dance past him.'

Marianne cringes. But then she gets hold of herself, heroically. Crying is out of the question, you simply cannot cry black mascara tears. Wolf plays his part well, he holds her tightly in his arms, and as they dance past the pirate he gives a relaxed wave and calls out, 'Hallo *old boy*,' putting emphasis on the 'old'. The pirate glances over again, rattled.

I take in my surroundings. Suddenly I am flooded with the feeling of being young, the feeling that we are young, Marianne, Wolf and I. Young, and in spite of it all unspoilt. They both wave at me, Marianne looks enchanting, she's thrown her head back, she dances wonderfully, defiantly, and Wolf too is looking attractive, confidence-inspiring, sweet, all cleaned up. Who knows whether anyone else notices, whether the women who want to whisk TAM TAM away in their LaSalles see that something is happening here in front of them, that someone—even if it is just a silly little girl—is being cured of something—even if it is only a silly little passion, while the band plays 'Happy Days'.

Gradually the place fills up. There are fine ladies who look expensive and who fall, not always clearly on one side or the other, into two categories: 'we pay for ourselves' and 'we are paid for'. And there are nightmares, scarecrows plucked straight from the hedge. The music is genuinely captivating. It's youthful, winsome, boisterous. The violinist also plays clarinet, the drummer also plays the saxophone, the pianist can sing. If the party gradually degenerates into an orgy, it's these three who'll be responsible, more than the alcohol. The clarinetist, with a figure like the poet Eichendorff, tall, blond and slim, climbs around on the tables and benches while playing, he scrambles like a sleepwalker through the room, he lures people from their tables like a rat-catcher, the most blasé among them put down their cigarettes; and the mating call reaches the scarecrows too, like a signal to forget their unloveliness and inhibitions. A gray old lady steps up to dance a solo jig, hair over her face in disarray, two steps forward, two steps back, then in a circle, the way children dance. She knots up her skirt and smiles like a ballerina, she kicks up her short legs, everyone claps in time with the rhythm. An even older partner is scared up for a spectral minuet to music from the fiddler, who's now standing on the piano, his face nearly gone in the clouds of smoke gathering toward the ceiling. He hovers gently, sweetly, high above the riotous dance hall, like an angel still half stuck in the clouds.

'Did you see the woman who throws bombs?' asks Wolf.

'What?'

'That liberated older lady. She's said to have thrown bombs in New York as propaganda, I'm not sure if it was for the Communists or to protest the war. Either way. Marianne, now it's your turn to stay at our table and flirt as shamelessly as you can with that guy, across from you. Tonight you look only at very young, pretty men. Otherwise, it's not exactly the right medicine for our old friend.'

Wolf and I dance. He points out this and that for me—Kiki, for example, the starlet of Montmartre, now faded and fat, who looks like a marzipan pig, shakes her hips obscenely, beckons to men, rolls around the room, ruined and melting, a wax figure someone has exposed to high heat. A young woman, tender as a bluebell, suddenly decides to air out her triangular top—all you have to do is untie the ends of the kerchief at the back—and then uses it to fan herself. The whole room can see her tender breasts, and no one is bothered in the least.

'Wolf,' I ask, 'for God's sake, what sort of people are these?'

'That one?' asks Wolf, as usual as full of concern for anyone else as for me. 'That poor girl—some painter's model from Paris with lung disease, she doesn't have long to live.' And he gravely gestures a greeting over to her, respectfully, as though doffing his cap to a coffin.

The pirate is dancing now too with his voluptuous girl, he dances in high style, a very slow tango, strictly matched to the rhythm. He's a large man—many a medal could find a home across his broad chest—but he prefers being king of Saint-Tropez to being a reputable club member in his English homeland.

'Look at that,' says Wolf, 'what a handsome couple. That's just how I've always imagined natural selection works. Go on now, be fruitful and multiply.'

I turn round.

It's not possible. I stare in horror at you and the Blonde, then drag Wolf toward the door, just to be out of here, keep fleeing till we reach the safety of the stacked barrels outside. And I sit down on one of the barrels, ball up my fists desperately and tell myself: I won't cry, I won't cry, I won't.

Those next moments I'll never forget: the smell of tar and fetid harbor water, the urgent, barbaric, repetitive dance-hall music, the harbor lights twinkling red and green, masts gently swaying against the sky, and there I am in the midst of all this—shaken by the fever of an awful sickness, shaken by jealousy, insane, animal jealousy. My only desire is to destroy, the woman, the man, and myself, yes myself also, just to rip myself to shreds, dash myself against the rocks, as though no other freedom were imaginable, the only choice to extinguish, cut at the root, exterminate. I've known nothing till now like this dark rage, this dark wave that submerges me utterly, I've never imagined that such things were waiting inside me, or that they could be released from one second to the next, all because you danced by with the Blonde.

'Wolf, I'm sorry but I've got to go home. I have to go home, right now. I don't feel well. Please excuse me. I just have to get out of here.'

'First let's take a minute to walk it off,' says Wolf. 'Or you can sit where you are if you like. But you can't go home. I'm not letting you go in this state.'

'Wolf,' I say, 'what I'd like most is to die. I mean that literally. To fall down somewhere, anywhere, where it's dark, and just be gone. You really think she is that beautiful?'

'Yes,' says Wolf. 'That much you can't change.'

It would be a great comfort if I could somehow just lower her. But there's nothing to be done. Wolf is quite right. She is undeniably beautiful. They're a handsome couple, were Wolf's words, I turn this over in my heart and it hurts, deeply and slowly and penetratingly, all the way to my fingernails and the ends of each hair, a highly sophisticated pain.

'It's the bouillabaisse man, isn't it?'

'There's only the bouillabaisse man, I'm afraid.'

'He looks good. How'd he suddenly show up here?'

I'd like to know that too. Bit by bit Wolf draws me out with questions, loosens me up, gets me to talk until it feels natural to talk about you. But he isn't indulgent. He refuses to let me get sentimental.

'You need to put it behind you,' he says at last. 'Everyone does. These ups and downs, they can happen—they have to happen, that's what keeps life interesting. And you've basically been coping well with this until tonight's setback. Look, I'm not one for heroism, swords and hand grenades and all that, but the way Marianne danced past the pirate with me, I thought that was grand. But if you were to kill yourself, or even if you just want to kill yourself, that I do not find so grand. If you want to have a good cry, you're certainly entitled to. Here's my handkerchief. But don't take too long, please. People always seem to think it's ecstasy to wallow in misery. You should see just once what it's like not to wallow. What it's like when you have every reason to be unhappy, and you just refuse. That's what I call a real rush, that's a fantastic feeling, when you can carry yourself, all alone. That's what you should try. Not everyone can see it through. But I'd bet on you to do it, absolutely.'

'But I love him, Wolf,' I say.

'So what, kid, so what.' And he whistles impatiently, *I love him in the morning and I love him in the night.*

'I want to go home, Wolf,' I say.

'Out of the question. Cowards run. You can't always be running from that man. These encounters could start happening more often now. Chin up, show some composure, kid. Now we're going back in to Marianne. She's in there sitting on the grill as we speak, just like you. We can't just walk out on her.'

Wolf will not relent. He hauls me back between the gaping villagers in the brightly lit hall. The musicians are playing 'It Only Happens Once, and It'll Never Come Again.' The sweet, sappy music drips from the angelic fiddler's violin, hot wax on my heart and Marianne's. Commander Wolf has marshaled his wayward troops to stand and fight, and he compels me to dance in the face of my foe. He holds me with care, I move as though in a dream, the mirror shows me a slender silhouette, a severe profile—'Try to look pleasant,' Wolf whispers, 'one, two, three'—and we've glided past your table as though there had never in the world been such a thing as love, separation, pain, only the movement, the sound, the spell of this moment.

'Good girl,' says Wolf like a dentist. 'See, that wasn't so bad. Mind you don't keep stepping on my toes. I don't deserve that from you.'

I smile at him. All my tender gratitude, everything that is never acknowledged aloud between us, is wrapped in this smile like tissue paper, and I hope he'll take it. He gets so distracted sometimes.

'Wolf, he's seen me. No, now he's seen me, he's looking at us.'

'Let him,' says Wolf, and holds me more tightly in his arms. He throws himself into the dance, sings along, first at a low hum then louder, he tries to carry me with him into the fray.

Marianne has been busy in our absence. She looks rather feverish but it suits her, and she's laughing loudly with a hand-some young blond man who looks like the Prince of Wales.

This dance has to end, like all the others. Even though the violinist, with angelic mercy, clairvoyantly tacked on a da capo. We have to return to our table. Marianne steps up and asks, 'Where have you been?' But without waiting for an answer she goes on, 'There are some new people here worth meeting,' nodding over at your table. Now I realize that the Prince of Wales is one of your party. 'I've been dancing this whole time with that handsome young man, the pirate's having a fit.'

I turn my back to you. I recite poetry, *Guter Mond, du gehst so stille*, and *Müde bin ich, geh zur Ruh*—while Marianne and Wolf chatter. If only the music would start up again, throw a blanket over reality. Anything so I wouldn't have to sit around like this, naked and exposed. *Hab ich Unrecht heut getan, lieber Gott sieh es nicht an.* Just this once to be back in my childhood bed, this once to be born again, a new person.

'Let's go,' you say. You grab my arm, I follow you, we walk quickly out of the noise into the open air. Once again I'm sitting trembling on a barrel, once again the harbor lights are twinkling, only it's completely different this time. I can tell you are furious. You pace with long strides back and forth in front of me, then come to a halt and say:

'Why did you run away? Aren't you ashamed of yourself?'

Suddenly I am absolutely calm. I know that you will grab me and shake me and I'll simply look at you without fear, just look at you. And that is exactly what happens.

'You—' you say, '—you should be ashamed', and here you give me a shake, 'for the way you behaved.'

I just look back at you.

'So that's it, you're not afraid of me?' you ask, furious.

I'm not, truly. Why should I be? Before, yes, I was afraid. Now that you're grabbing me and shaking me, now that you're in a rage and acting like a complete stranger, I'm not afraid at all. Now I'm in the thick of this; the hard part was approaching it.

'I said all I had to say in my note,' I say after a while, in an amazingly calm voice, neither too soft nor too shrill.

'That scrap,' you say fiercely, 'that frigid, stupid scrap of paper. It was ludicrous, do you understand? Witless and unimaginative. Naturally, you never imagined what it's like to come home and order a special meal for the room, have flowers in one's arms and a plan in the works for the next morning about where we'll drive together, to do whatever you'd enjoy most— the Mortola Garden, maybe. Yes, to come back home, and I don't mean the hotel, I mean you, you fool, and find the hotel room dark and silent as a funeral and this stupid scrap of paper, and in the next room it's empty, just your slippers left behind, untidy as always. And I picked them up and I threw them at the wall, and then I wept, if you must know, and went to the doorman to see if there was anything that could be done, if I could follow you like a lunatic, but he just smirked and claimed to know nothing. Then I got to go to bed and worry about you, you may not believe it but I was worried sick, knowing how your high blood pressure can affect you. And the whole next day I called around like a madman, to Munich and Berlin, no one knew a thing about you. Until finally Erich wrote me a card.'

'I'm sorry,' I say. I really am. 'But I couldn't have imagined any such reaction, truly.'

'Because you're a fool,' you say.

Now I gradually become angry too. Of course I am the only one who's guilty, I think bitterly.

'I couldn't have imagined it, because actually you did everything you possibly could to make me leave. I didn't leave for my own amusement. You think I enjoyed running away? What, you don't think you badgered me into leaving? Or that you yourself weren't unimaginative? Quite a lot has to happen before a woman leaves, we're taught to be patient, and yes, we've learnt to tolerate an awful lot, you've methodically hardened us. I've been in bad shape too, my dear, I've withstood fears of my own and had my own sleepless nights. But now I'm doing well. Very well, even.'

The 'very well' is triumphant. In this moment, some part of me takes vengeance for Eva and Adelheid and Marianne, all rivals and all sisters.

'I can get by alone, too,' I say, and pound on the barrel with my fist; it doesn't sound hollow, thank God, not the barrel, and not my voice either.

'Then why were you in such a hurry to replace me?'

'Are you jealous? So soon?' I ask, enjoying the fact that for once this damning accusation falls on you. You've reminded me often enough of my own shortcomings, in just the same way.

Disappointingly, you don't pursue it.

'He looks nice enough, your young man, maybe a bit pro-vincial, but at least you seem to have landed in clean hands. I'm glad of that, at least.'

Now I'm furious. Patronizing, condescending, that's the new tone. 'He's enchanting. And so marvelously young.'

'Do you love him?' you ask, suddenly turning serious.

For a whole minute I wait to answer. For a whole minute I have an overpowering desire to throw my arms around your neck, to say to you that it's to you and only you I belong hopelessly, inescapably, that nothing can change that, not in fourteen days, not in fourteen years. Why don't you know it? Here you are in front of me, no more than a few feet away. I could touch your face, take it so tenderly in my hands. You're so close, and proximity pulls me toward you unbearably; it would be so lovely to fall, to give in, but then everything would be lost again.

You're looking at me. The old magic still works. I'm paralyzed. I feel at the same time nearness and distance, attraction and resistance, attachment and separateness. I think of Adelheid, Eva and Marianne, I summon them like patron saints in this dark hour, and then I say with finality: 'I love him.' Differently of course, so differently, as you love a brother, but you don't need to know that. So now you are further from me than ever.

'That was fast,' you say. Now you look tired and low.

'You never took too long to think it over yourself.'

'That may be true, but it's painful too. I know you won't believe it. But I really did count on you. I thought you were patient, that you understood. Doubtless it was asking too much. I was thoughtless and tormented you; then you tormented me. And now we have nothing more to reproach one another with. Except that I took the first step, I suppose. Forgive me.'

So that's what it comes down to. Evening the score. Pain for pain, desertion for desertion. It's all worked out.

We look at one another once more. I can still take everything back. If only you had come alone, I think. If I start over now, I have to compete with the Blonde, who dances so well. A handsome couple. I have no fight left in me. I only have an aching need for peace.

You turn and walk away. A few more steps and the music from the dance hall absorbs you into it, the lights and the heavy fog of wine. I watch you as one watches a ship leaving from the harbor to go to America. It gets there sooner than you might think.

Then I run, I run like an insane person, first through the town, then out on the country roads. There are no street lights, nothing but the eyes of alley cats glinting in the dark. The country roads at night bring on a calm. The view of the bay, the Massif des Maures, the great wide sky, the fitful streaks of light from the beacon at Cap Camarat that keeps crossing my path, all these are trusted friends guiding me by the arm.

It's wonderful to be alone. Each step away from the houses brings release. I get the desire to go for a swim. I clamber down the rocky path to the small inlet. The water is a lusterless black, except in one small section where it reflects the bright floodlights from the nearby house belonging to Colette. They cast light like a sign across the sea, so calm here it could be a lake. What does the sign mean, I wonder? Finally I reach the dock. It feels magnificent to strip off my clothes, to feel cool wind on my hot skin, magnificent to dive in, to go under, to rinse everything away, everything that's heavy on my head and heart. It's wonderful to lie on my back weightless, to have the stars above me, my eyes tracing the dark outline of the headland, to find my way back to my own measure in this great dark unpeopled world. It's like a game you might play in a dream. Small waves make a ruffled collar around my neck, play with me.

Gradually I become aware of the cold. I have no towel so I dry myself with my shirt and put on only my linen pants. I hold the damp shirt in my hand. It's night, no one is around. I run to keep warm. My skin burns. It's magnificent to feel skin, body, the muscles in my legs, to run into the wind, to make my wet hair fly. The seaweed yields under my feet, soft and elastic. Sometimes I slip back into the water. The hemp soles of my espadrilles are soaked. I pull them off and run barefoot. The pain feels good. I want to go anywhere but home. I want to run half naked all the way to Cap Saint-Pierre, right up to the huge cliffs, where the real ocean lies open before you. And lay myself down there, in some small rocky bay, to sleep. I run still further, instead of turning toward my house I run until the beacon light from Colette's house falls across me. Light brings me back to my senses.

I turn back slowly, deflated, my ecstatic rush suddenly falls away, my limbs are unbearably painful, pebbles pierce into my bare feet. Gingerly I feel my way back to the cottage. Soon it smells not like salt, seaweed, ocean but like thyme and mint. Here I'm at home, I grow calm and quiet. Colette climbs down the plane tree, flings herself down to meet me. She's night-crazed, she dances around the well, plays with the small branches lying on the ground, rips towels down from the laundry line, resists my attempts to catch her, hides herself behind the flowerpots and hunts madly through the vine stocks, until at last, without taking notice of her or calling her, I go into the house quietly; I leave the door ajar. Then she sneaks in after me and gets into her basket. I'm hardly in bed when she's there climbing around on my face, she burrows under the covers, attacks my toes, and finally, gradually, she calms down and snuggles into her favorite spot between my neck and shoulder. Her whiskers tickle but she won't stand for being moved, she starts to purr loudly and we both fall asleep just as we are.

We're driving up a wide, steep road. To our right and left stand whitewashed cypresses. Someone sits between us, but I can't tell who. We are driving with the lights off. You say: 'Someone is visiting tomorrow. You won't be able to eat with us.' So I go to a café. I'm sad I can't even eat with you now. Wolf is sitting at the next table but he doesn't recognize me. He spends the whole time drawing on the tablecloth. If only the waitress won't notice! I wave at him to cut it out, but he keeps drawing. He's drawing boats but they have trees instead of masts, and from their huge treetops you can hear birds singing.

Then we are driving again past the cypress trunks. The car takes a sharp curve. The door leaps open and I fall out. You keep driving. I want to run after you but I can't. An old woman comes up the cypress boulevard, she walks behind me with a big cane. I climb up a tree trunk. She strikes the tree with her cane calling, 'Come down!' But that's impossible. I'm wearing nothing but a nightgown. The old woman knocks impatiently and so powerfully that the tree begins to sway dangerously. I hold tight and know that if she keeps this up I'll fall.

I sit straight up in bed. Colette, too, is awake. She stands on the pillow next to me, her eyes shining in the darkness. There must be someone at the front door. I'm terribly frightened. I don't move for a full minute. The knocking keeps getting louder. Someone rattles the door.

'Who's there?' I call out. In my terror I forget to speak French. But whoever is outside understands me.

'Please, open the door—I've been knocking for a quarter of an hour!'

It's you—YOU—here, in the middle of the night. I leap up, rush to the hall and throw back the bolt. There you are. I stand in the doorway for a moment, not letting you in, and ask:

'What do you want, for God's sake?'

You push me inside, however, shut the door, lock it again, and say:

'Back into bed with you. Barefoot on a cold stone floor, naturally. You'll catch your death.' And you corral me back into my room.

Colette is standing there on the bed, yawning and wide-eyed, her tail curled in a question mark.

'What do you want?'

'Cover up, you'll catch cold.' You walk over to the chimneypiece and light two more candles.

'It's nice in here,' you say, looking around, 'really quite charming. The one thing missing is a good desk to keep some order. We can go get one together tomorrow.'

'Are you completely insane?'

'Why have you started lying?' you ask. 'I've never known you to be a liar before.'

'Because I wanted peace and quiet,' I say. 'And anyway, it wasn't a lie. I—' and then I turn over in the bed and sob. You pay no attention.

'A fine cat,' you say. 'Much better to keep a cat than a lover.'

'Give her to me!' I snatch Colette from you furiously. 'That's *my* cat. What on earth are you thinking, anyway? Why are you here? I didn't invite you. I only want peace, that's all, finally just some peace and quiet…'

'Wolf is really a charming young man,' you say. 'We got along wonderfully. Discreet and sensible. He even accompanied me here. I would never have found this place on my own. He may join us tomorrow for breakfast. I hope that's all right with you. And then we can all drive together to Nice. I've invited Marianne as well. That girl needs some distraction.'

'Oh!' I say. 'This shamelessness is a new low. You genuinely do not seem to grasp that I have my own life now. I'm not going back to Nice! I'm staying here. This cottage is mine for three months.'

You inspect the room, and then begin to unpack your things. This I recognize. Orderly, methodical. A prelude to sleep. You set out your watch, money, passport and wallet on the mantel. And then you start to remove your clothes. I watch, bewildered.

'But I never invited you,' I say, weakly.

'A regrettable oversight. I've always said it: you neglect essentials. But in the end, I know you too well. I've already washed my hands outside. My neck too. Wolf was good enough to draw some water from the well for me. An amiable, obliging young man.'

You're nearly undressed.

'Hold on,' I say emphatically. 'It's not that simple.'

'Oh,' you say, 'but it is that simple. Move over.'

'But this is not what I want,' I say.

'Do we really have to keep talking about it?' you say. 'We tried talking before. Nothing came of it but nonsense. Now, do you want me to freeze?'

I hate you. Grudgingly, I turn to the wall. I take up as little of the bed as I can.

'Saint Julian the Hospitable,' you say, taking up most of the bed as though it were the most natural thing in the world. You've blown out the candles on the mantelpiece. You've locked the outside door. Colette is lying on the pillow between us. She's a French cat: nothing shocks her. Then you blow out the last of the candles.

I hate you. Your breath comes loud and unconcerned. Soon, I know, your hand will wander over. It starts with the hair. It seems harmless, almost fraternal. You rely on my weakness. It's all been admirably staged. Night-time and solitude, candles blown out, only one bed. Whether I like it or not, here we are under the same covers. After that, the rest is practically scripted.

And there's your hand, right on schedule; as predicted, the hypocrite's touching my hair. I sit up angrily and yell: 'Hey! Cut that out. No more of that, or I'll spend the night in the village. Kindly keep your hands to yourself. Who knows who that hand has been stroking since the last time I saw you.'

'Nonsense,' you say, 'utter nonsense. Sleep tight, you goose. And if I happen to kick you during the night, let's not jump to conclusions, I'm not trying to make a pass at you.'

You turn over, three times, four, like a dog looking for the right place to sleep. The bed creaks. Finally, peace. Your back is turned to me, with your legs familiarly splayed clear across the bed, and I see where I am. Total unconcern; despicable intimacy, despicable warmth. But, I swear to myself, this once and never again. I'll let myself be blindsided once—twice, never. I wait listening for you to fall asleep. Your breath becomes even as you sink deeper. It comes slower, more unconsciously. Stray words surface from your dream-like bubbles. Thank God, you're asleep at last. I'm alone again.

I lie on my back, pressed close to the wall. I'll never get to sleep like this. I'm determined not to touch your body, even in my dreams. I've spent the last fourteen days making my way up a mountain; at first it was hard work, then it became a pleasure. Now suddenly the mountain is caving in under my feet and I'm dangerously near where I set out from. I don't want to go back there: jealousy, humiliation. I have no desire to be shaken anymore, like tonight. I want my paradise back, paradise before the creation of Adam. The rib has made herself self-sufficient. I can still feel the water and wind on my skin and the sharp stones under my feet.

Colette has disappeared. No doubt we were too noisy for her. I feel around the pillow carefully, accidentally brush against your hair. She's gone. I'm pleased that she does not want to spend the night in bed with you.

Tomorrow you'll drive to Nice, I think with relief. At least you can't drag me there along with you by force. Tomorrow this derailed train car can get back on its tracks. Or so I think to myself, with desperate confidence.

You lie next to me breathing softly. Asleep, you are disarmed; I want to hate you, but now it's not so easy. I know exactly how you look. A little bit foolish, like all sleepers. No longer the self-possessed gentleman, no more self-assurance or certainty of success. You have your mouth open a little, your hair has strayed across your forehead. You're small, I think, very small. As though sensing these thoughts, you pull your long limbs in closer, collecting what you've scattered, you curl yourself into a fetal position, cut off from the world, all helplessness, resting from your forty-year journey.

Something rustles at the window. It's a restless night. Maybe the neighbor's dog. Suddenly the white curtains flutter open. I hear a scratching inside now. An ashtray clinks on the window ledge. My only thought is it's a good thing you're here—I grab hold of you and shake you out of your deep sleep, feel around past you for the matches and candle. I've struck a flame before you know where you are. Colette is hanging on the window ledge, looking startled and guilty, caught in the act of sneaking in from a night-time excursion. She's tangled herself in the mosquito netting and now she can't move, whichever way she tries. She's soon rescued. I make excuses on her behalf.

'She's hardly ever done this before. She doesn't usually escape at night. She just didn't like you being here.'

'Mmm,' you say, still sleep-drunk.

Carefully I climb over you back into bed, you mountain of a man, holding Colette in my arm. I set her down by the wall, not between us as before. Then I ask you politely to blow out the candle.

'Would you hand her to me, please,' is your reply.

I hand you the animal, now purring merrily. In your large hands she looks three weeks old again. I've never seen you play with animals. Colette scratches you, bites and hangs on fiercely to your finger with her sharp little teeth; then she walks around on your face, surveys the new terrain, gently bats at the hill of your nose and suddenly bites your chin, like a good predator. I marvel that you let all this happen. Occasionally you let out an 'Ouch!' and shake her off, but ever so softly, gently. Your shadow darts over the opposite wall, cast long beyond the bedspread. You've taken possession of the room completely, you and your shadow.

Colette has grown tired. She lies down in the warm cave between neck and shoulder, pushing her head up under your chin.

'Now you've cast your spell over her too,' I say. 'She's only a woman after all. What a pity.'

'Well, what do you want her to be?'

'A virgin Amazon who bites and scratches men. Put out the candle.'

'Last time I got the candle part all wrong. It's not proper to put the light out too soon. Night-time is only for lovers and intimates. But it's made you stubborn and suspicious. Did you hate me very much?'

'Oh yes. And don't imagine it's over just yet.'

'But it is,' you say, calm. 'Look at me. It's in the past.' And then gently, without any air of possessiveness, you lay your arm around me, pull me toward you, and make space for my head in the hollow of your right shoulder, while Colette occupies the left. I want to be on my guard. But something—I don't know whether it's fatigue, the soft candlelight, your calming warmth or simply a fateful sense that it has to be—something disarms me. Just once I sigh deeply, exhale all the tension, all resistance with that one breath, you extinguish the candle as though it was my sigh that put it out, and the night starts over new.

I wake up. I could almost believe last night was a ghostly visitation. The sunlight spills across the room as usual. The men's clothes, money, watch, papers have all disappeared. Maybe a genie brought you here for one night, like in a fairy tale, laid you down beside me and then spirited you away again. I'm inclined to believe anything rather than the probable. But a look through the window brings you back to me. Under the plane tree the garden table has been spread with my favorite cloth, the green-and-gold-checked one. So, we have the same taste. And there you are, carefully carrying plates and cups, Colette following at your heels. Maybe you really are a good person. Maybe all you need is a new climate and time of day to unfold differently. Maybe you're like my element, water, able to pour yourself into any new jug. Maybe I didn't do you justice when I wrote: Your life is not my life, your home is not my home, your language is not my language. Maybe you don't have any such clear-cut life, or solid-built home, maybe you have more than one language. I saw you as red, called you red, and acted as though red wasn't for me. But maybe like a mirror you have no color of your own and only reflect back what's in front of you, sometimes red, sometimes yellow, sometimes green, and now, as you set the table outside, blue, because blue is my favorite color. I thought you were unfaithful, unprincipled, without conscience. But maybe none of that was true. Maybe the truth is that inconstancy is your character, and colorlessness your color. Maybe you're being faithful to yourself only when you're unfaithful.

Maybe I understand you better having lived awhile by the water. It's in its nature to change with the weather, to grow opaque or glitter along with the sky. It's in its nature that it can't be held too close, that it slips away from your grasping hand in a thousand tiny droplets. But when you trust it, when you feel devotion in place of fear, when you take the waves in your arms and float gently on the surface, when you find your balance and steady your breath, it carries you. Then it's softer than any bed standing on solid ground.

I quickly pull on my swimsuit and come outside. A full bucket of water is warming in the sun by the well. And you're plucking the last ripe apricots from the boughs I can't get to, reaching up to them with your long arms.

We eat a breakfast of fruit and tea and buttered bread and mountain honey, *miel de l'esterel*, full of the scent of thyme and lavender. Colette washes herself on the well. The tall grass tickles our bare legs. The air is full of wasps and butterflies.

Small lizards go walking around the walls of the house. It starts to get wonderfully warm. The sky is a vault so serene, so blue, so clear that I want to sing or cry. Will you feel it too? Or perhaps I'm mistaken, and you'll drive to Nice and walk on paved streets, and you'll see only the houses and not the sky.

'I'm driving to Nice this afternoon,' you say.

'What?' I ask, in disbelief.

'That's right. Are you coming?'

No, not I. It will always be too soon to leave this behind.

'You're in a hurry,' I say. 'You won't be this close to the earth again anytime soon. But maybe that's not so important to you.' And I bite into an apricot that smells like primroses, an apricot that tastes like it smells, full of sap and sweetness.

'I just have to go get my things. And say a few farewells. I was a bit abrupt last night. Honestly, I'll be glad when I can put it all behind me.'

So that's what you meant. I hand you half my apricot as though offering half a kingdom. You take it, kissing my hand, and at last we understand one another. Then you help me wash the dishes.

'How do you like my place?' I ask. My place: I savor the sound.

'Funny,' you say, 'that you of all people should have made yourself independent. A little field mouse like you! I like it, I like it much more than I can say. I've seldom liked anything so much. If it suits you I think we should stay a good long while. Even the kitchen's in good order. I didn't know you had it in you.'

We go for a long walk. I show you everything, yes *I* show *you*. And you observe and admire. The agave flowers and the oleander, the zigzag path to the Cap, my private beach where we now go for a swim and sunbathe, naked as God made us.

'You've made yourself still more beautiful,' you say. 'Not such a field mouse after all. Now you look more like an Arabian boy.'

Here, I continue to enjoy my triumphs. I swim better than you, surer and faster, with more real joy. I submerge my head under every fresh wave. I can dive and do somersaults. Then we lay ourselves out under the sun on great flat stones and bake. We oil each other up solemnly, diligently, methodically, first the front, then the back.

'Now I'm realizing for the first time how much I missed you,' I say. 'I never could reach the spot back there.'

The sun broods over us. Every pore is saturated. You hum lazily from time to time and turn this way and that. Finally we reel back home woozily, sun-drunk.

'So,' I say, 'now what do you want to do?'

'Lie in the shade and finish sweating.'

That you can. Meanwhile I gather eggs and tomatoes and a few figs. In the kitchen I find a package from Wolf. Inside are sardines. On the outside he's painted a beautiful picture, a table covered with peas, artichokes, apricots, cherries, figs. In front of the table stands a man who looks a little like you, with a speech banner that says: *I'm looking for something to chew on*. Underneath is written, 'There's more in this life than just fruit to eat, the time comes when a man just has to have meat. Yours, with love, Wolf.'

We eat a terrific meal. A tomato omelet and a golden-brown heap of fried sardines tossed with fennel and parsley.

'This life is ridiculously good,' you say as the last sardine tail disappears with a crackle between your teeth. 'If you keep me here any longer, I'll grow a coat of fur or roots and leaves, and I'll leave my human shape behind once and for all. Meanwhile in Berlin, they're sitting around at desks, on the telephone.'

'When do you drive to Nice?'

'Tomorrow.'

'What about your things?'

'We can go buy a swimsuit and toothbrush. Maybe I'll drive the day after tomorrow. Or in two weeks. It doesn't matter much anymore.'

Then you sleep. I clean up on tiptoe. No one comes to disturb us. Silence hangs over the cottage like a spell. Even the guinea fowl know better than to cackle. At four I wake you with a cup of tea. You sit up and look at me, straight out of some other dream, intent and bewildered.

'Dear child,' you say then, 'I think it's better that I drive to Nice today after all.'

'It's already quite late,' I say.

'I need to set things straight. I can't go around leaving chaos in my wake. You know what I mean. I have to let her know, at least. Surely you agree?'

'Is it so simple?'

You shrug your shoulders.

'You're letting yourself take the easy way out.'

'The easy way out this time is also the natural path. What else should I do?'

Strictly speaking, there's plenty you could do. But at the moment you have no desire to argue with me about it. You dress silently and hastily, embrace me on your way out, and utter those words men always say: 'Don't wait up for me.'

I watch you go. What else is there for me to do? We stick to tradition. You don't look back. You don't whistle or stroll like Wolf, you push forward with impatient, quick steps toward the oncoming hours.

The tea sits undrunk, and has to be tossed out on the grass. I make myself busy. It's not likely you'll get back tonight. It's eighty kilometers to Nice, a mountain road full of switchbacks, no good for night driving. I hope you stay there overnight and don't race back like a man possessed. And yet I'm afraid of what will happen if you stay.

Wolf and Marianne arrive just as I make up my mind, uneasy and full of nerves, to head into the village.

'He just drove off,' Marianne calls out to me. 'We saw him. It looked like he was in a huge rush. Why did you let him go? You shouldn't have let him out of your sight, I know the type.'

'If he doesn't come back, then we're better off without him, isn't that right, Colette?' says Wolf.

Marianne is up in arms.

'You're an underhanded, two-faced person after all that, aren't you. I have every right to be furious with you. For the last fourteen days you let me think you were a virgin! I don't call that a very respectable way to behave.'

I apologize. I make fresh tea. We sit on the grass companionably.

'For our dear Marianne this development is a genuine blessing,' says Wolf. 'In the long term, it's no good only being interested in your own love life. It spoils your character. *Look at me, kid.*'

'When will he be back?' asks Marianne.

'No idea.'

'But you have to ask men these things!'

'My dear, you absolutely must never ask men these things. You're missing the most basic fundamentals. He probably doesn't even know himself. You can't live with a watch in your hand. You have a lot to learn, sweet Marianne. You have to give men space to move around in,' and Wolf makes a capacious hand gesture, 'space,' he repeats dreamily, 'the more the better.'

'And what if that space is full of other women?'

'That happens, of course,' says Wolf. 'In German we just call that fate. Everything that happens is fate.'

Marianne is glowing with curiosity. She's most interested in the Blonde.

'She was awfully sore last night. I saw the whole thing, first-hand. Her boyfriend disappeared all of a sudden with Wolf. Then she watched the clock and when a quarter of an hour had passed she left. In a hurry. That woman has principles. Well, she can afford to have them: beautiful women are always the most sensitive.'

'Let's hope she really sticks it to him,' says Wolf. 'Nothing's worse than being suddenly forgiven. Just when it's time for something to end and the future's finally opening up again, that's when they generously put you back in chains.'

Marianne continues: 'Of course, a fifteen-minute limit is low. Me, I would have waited another fifty, in smaller increments of course. But it would have been in vain. It was a most educational evening.' After a pause she suddenly says, 'But aren't you going crazy with jealousy? He's driving to her right now, you know he is!'

'Marianne, my dear,' says Wolf, 'you have too much imagination. And not enough tact. You'll have to learn to balance the two out.' And then he puts an arm round me and says:

'You were right. I think he's terrific. You might still experience something remarkable with him. But that's not what really matters. What matters is who makes you happy or unhappy. That's all. And here you've made a good choice. I have to say, he made an impression on me yesterday. Like some great ravenous, powerful predator. Like a superb tomcat, playing with mice. An ideal challenge for a tamer of wild animals, which is really what you women are good at. There are lots of people who have to think first before they do anything, and they just feel wretched all the time. Then they mostly sit around thinking so long they never make up their minds to do anything at all.'

'Those are inhibitions,' says Marianne.

'Yes, but you see,' says Wolf, 'inhibited people will call him uninhibited. But I love it. It's only really secure people who walk safe without reins.'

Marianne says, 'Actually, that's all just nonsense. What matters is that you love him, and that you try to find a way to make it last as long as possible. But it's up to the stars in the end. Maybe now your stars are lining up. What concerns me, meanwhile, is that my stars are terrible. Mars always gets in the way for me. What do you think *I* should do now?'

'You should read a good book for a change,' says Wolf. 'First things first, we have to find you a cottage of your own. A woman belongs in a home, not a hotel room.'

We decide to go for an evening walk. As soon as the day starts to wind down, Marianne grows melancholy. Wolf whistles and is distracted. I think of you and how by now you will have arrived in Nice. We walk by the water along a narrow rocky path. To our right the sea shimmers under a fiery evening sky. To our left the shore climbs steeply up to a hilltop. We pass stretches of vineyard and walk under dark stands of pine. Scattered over the hill there are several houses, and Wolf decides this is where Marianne should live.

'Look, Marianne darling, what you need is to take the longer view. In every sense.'

Marianne isn't convinced. 'Up here? All alone? There are definitely snakes hiding in those bushes.'

'Yes,' says Wolf, 'as alone as you can get. We can't let the fashion for lady hermits die out. Someone has to fly the flag high in the name of tradition. It's a Saint-Tropez legacy. Now it's your turn. Just think how relaxing it will be for you. Imagine what it will feel like to have no one yelling at you. You can get up when you like. You don't have to make coffee anymore. You don't even have to eat breakfast if it doesn't bring you pleas-ure. You don't have to watch the clock, and you don't have to wait up. Lunch will never get cold again. What is wrong with men, anyway? In general, they're mostly unbearable. Because they slept badly or they have toothache. Suddenly they find themselves confronting their own mortality or they recognize their own genuine mediocrity. Then it's you that has to talk them down. That's really what you're there for, it turns out. To comfort and admire. So darling, you'll be amazed what it's like to live alone. It's going to be a great adventure for you.'

'Wolf is quite right,' I say. 'It is a great adventure. And when you have your own cottage, I'll visit you there, and you'll come visit us.' *Us*, I've said. The 'we' resurrected. Maybe too hastily, maybe too soon.

'Don't worry,' says Wolf, who catches everything, except when it's addressed to him directly. 'Don't waste your time thinking. The days will pass much more quickly.'

We are back at the village, a trio. We eat fried eggs at the Café de Paris and watch people. Everyone is there: TAM TAM with some new woman, the whiskey suicide, Kiki and the pirate. There they are, like actors in a play that's restaged, year after year, always the same. If I come back in a few years they'll all still be sitting here, straight out of the pages of the new season's theater review, positioned just so in the scenery of the harbor. Pascal the brown dog will carry his fleas and his hunger around from table to table, just to receive sugar packets or kicks, neither very good for him. Even Wolf and Marianne will always be there, the poor young painter and the petite young woman getting by on next to nothing. Maybe metamorphosed, under different names, a little less cheerful or less attractive, but in whatever shape they belong to this summer stock theater. You and I as well, we're nothing more or less than a pair of lovers in Saint-Tropez who arrive and fight and obey the landscape's demands. It's strange how easily the background becomes foreground here, how the backdrop takes precedence and the people become supporting figures. Only the village and the countryside are eternal here; in front of them the same feelings play out endlessly, independently of the players. Where I end, someone else will go on spinning out the thread, someone else will pick up the ball. Is it really so important whether you come back? Someone is always leaving, someone is always returning. Here, across from the pier, is where I first saw Marianne with the pirate, blissfully united. Here on this plaza is where I arrived alone and unhappy. It all seems so insignificant today. The game of love with its opposite poles, unhappy and happy, will continue to be played, because the landscape demands love. Saint-Tropez is like a music box that only knows one melody. It makes no difference who dances with whom to that melody, as long as the dance goes on.

I didn't wait up. Maybe that's why you've reappeared. I wake at the sound of your horn. You've driven the Buick boldly all the way up the reed path, now it's parked close to the house in the shadow of an oak. You heave two enormous suitcases from the trunk; it looks very permanent to me.

You're tired and battle-weary. 'I spent half the night packing,' you say.

'Was it very hard?' I ask.

You drag your suitcases into the kitchen with dogged determination. Then you want tea. We sit across from one another. You have new lines around your eyes. I get up again and give you a gentle kiss in the indentation at the nape of your neck, so slender and sweet. Your hair has recently begun to thin a little. In one spot the skin underneath gleams.

'I'm getting old,' you say.

'Yes,' I say, 'you're reaching the age when men are first capable of love, and worthy of love. You'll find it in Goethe.'

'Do you really think so?' you say, and you look at me almost pleadingly. You must really have had a wretched night.

'Someone told you otherwise?'

'Oh yes,' you say. 'It was rather dreadful. And I had promised her nothing, nothing of the kind. You know it's a matter of principle with me not to make that kind of promise. It just happened, a mutual kind of thing. Naturally I fell in love with her. You agree she's very pretty?'

'Wolf said you made a handsome couple.'

'Really, you should never have run off. It simply didn't have to happen at all. Some things have to happen, and other things you have some choice over. In this case, I had a choice. But I never felt obligated. I followed an appetite, and she did the same. We had a marvelous trip to Avignon. But we could never live together. You're the only one I want to live with. It's only with you I want to be at home. You're the only one I want to shave in front of. You have the most lovely eyes,' you suddenly say, 'only I think you cry too easily.'

'And was she very sad?' I ask.

'She was much too angry to be sad. Thank God. And I didn't leave time for a reconciliation. Tomorrow she'll go back to her husband. That's the good thing about married women. They don't throw themselves overboard, they just go back to being married. And so ends the chapter of "The Blonde Woman". It wasn't even very long. In school, they used to write at the end of my essays: "Does not complete assigned topic." But in the end the main theme here isn't "The Blonde Woman"; she was never more than a short chapter.'

You smile, and the lines on your face almost disappear. Then you stand and give me a kiss I'm very ready for. The Blonde will still sometimes come between us. I don't drop her as easily as you do. My jealousy is a better preservative than your love.

You throw yourself headlong into our new life. Everything has to be rearranged. New things must be bought. A desk for your elbows, because of course you can't write lying on your stomach as I do. That would be slovenly, and you like to maintain a manly order. Only chaotic people are so fussy. So we buy a desk where you can scatter your ashtray, file folder, calendar, notebook, watch and whatever else carries manly connotations. It takes me an extra half hour to tidy up and clean things. There are no two ways about it: you make a mess. Your big, heavy feet tread liberal quantities of dust and mud into the house.

Now we live together. You teach me punctuality and I take equal pains to improve your carelessness. Slowly you begin to misdate your letters. Slowly, it ceases to matter whether it's Wednesday or Friday. Even Sunday passes unnoticed in the general chaos. After all, the shops in the village stay open.

You seem happy to me. All you need now is to be; your life is uncomplicated. You're making up for a lost childhood, since by fourteen you had surely proved a prematurely accomplished student, craving girls and cigarettes. You get along with Wolf and you come with me on visits to Marianne's. Because now she has her own cottage, whitewashed like a hermit's cell, with the grand view prescribed by Wolf. We sit with her at her place, listen to gramophone records, and her little dog barks at the music. The dog is a present from Wolf, meant to eat the snakes in the bushes. But I don't believe there are any.

Marianne flirts with you a little, but half-heartedly, just the amount that's needed to bring life back into her.

Sometimes the four of us picnic together on the beach. Wolf brings his harmonica and sings the 'Song of the Loyal Hussar'. We build a fire under the pines and fry eggs and bacon, which taste gloriously of pine-cone smoke. We play catch in the water and dunk each other under, have splashing matches and race along the wet margin of sand by the ocean.

Sometimes the mistral comes and cools the water down and makes the air fresh again. The mistral is like a northern greeting, it keeps us from getting soft. It whips the sand up in our faces, the hair in our eyes, it pitches the excessively calm Mediterranean into manic convulsions and drives us all into mild delirium. On mistral mornings we drive with our friends to the bay with the widest mouth, someplace where the wind can dig deep into the water and pile up real waves that toss us around. We hold hands and run at the wall of water with giddy, euphoric unreason. There, someone will shout 'There's one'—and we hurl ourselves at the surge, a thrill takes hold of our hearts as the white-seamed colossus builds up and rolls closer, glassy, punishing, alive. We can't hear, we can't see, the saltwater in our eyes, the surf in our ears, it's as though we're baptized by the pounding blows, we lurch in the white foam, and the desire and fear renew themselves every time the water in front of us is replenished, blue-green with white veins, always another wave to drink us in, booming over us only to let us go, wash us away, cast us aside. This is the world's most blissful game, an eternal drowning, blinding, battering and getting back up. We can never have enough of it.

Afterwards we lie in a protected hollow out of the wind, no one speaks, we're out of breath. We gaze at the sky, feel our skin burn, feel the warm force of our blood pulsing through bodies that feel weakened yet inexplicably strengthened. Salt runs out of our hair, leaves white streaks on our foreheads, salt is everywhere, from our nostrils to deep in our throats. Tonight our kisses will taste of salt.

No one speaks anymore about personal problems. Like a giant blotting paper, the advancing summer sun has absorbed them. Even Marianne is noticeably quieter. Mostly we're preoc-cupied with living. Our bodies seem more important. We want to turn them brown as a hazelnut, healthy and smooth. We sleep long and deeply. We have no more arguments, miseries, tears. Now everyone adopts Wolf's ways, giving themselves over to the moment, to chance. No one mentions the future; its clouds never loom over us. Every day rises like water from the well, and we never think of testing how much is left.

Before this, did we ever really love one another? From five until six in the afternoon, or in the evening after the theater? Unthinkable. Unthinkable that life together could mean anything but shared days ending in shared nights. Unthinkable that we ever made plans according to the clock. Unthinkable to ever have eaten without hunger or drunk without thirst, according to the clock.

Now we bite into life. We soak ourselves full of sun like fruit. We stagger through summer and everything gets more gorgeous, less conscious. Time drips slowly but we don't count its drops. Every day the light's close is cut a little shorter, but we do as the farmers do, rise earlier and sleep earlier. Bit by bit summer changes into fall, but it doesn't break our hearts. We never get to the bottom of the cup. There are simply new fruits ripening now. Late figs bursting with sweetness on the trees, honey welling up from them like resin. Fleshy thick-skinned muscat grapes you can chew and fill up on, velvety dark-blue grapes whose juice you can drink like water. Every vine is heavy and laden with fruit, we pilfer some, no one minds. 'Go on then,' says the farmer woman, 'help yourself.' The farmer points us to the best vines.

Other landscapes produce milk, grains, cattle, lentils, all kinds of nourishment. This one makes wine and nothing but wine: fields full of vines, hills covered with vines, vines right up to the sand dunes, all to make wine not as precious commodity but in abundance, not for the cellar but for drinking like milk. Wooden crates, stacked high and leaning against one another like grape coffins soaked with dark juice, are driven in convoys to the wine press, their happy grave. Now it's all about the harvest, the sweat, barrels are sulfured and rolled out, the whole countryside is commotion, the streets are filled with wagons, everyone is on their feet.

Now we stay together on the vineyard all day and help. I develop a callus between thumb and forefinger where the shears press against my skin, and an unbearable ache in my back, to say nothing of the sore muscles in my legs. The grapes are never-ending. Row after row. White, pink, blue, black. Baskets are filled and emptied into boxes. Boxes are filled and brought to the wagon, no end in sight. We pick side by side into the same deep, round basket, that way the task goes more quickly.

When it gets cool in the evening and the fall humidity is rising from the soil we go for short walks, but our radius shrinks. Life is full right here. We no longer feel disquiet. We don't go forward, we don't go backward; we move back and forth. We embrace often, comfortable, unthinking embraces that pass into the innocence of sleep. Sometimes we're amazed at ourselves when a memory dawns on us of our past desire and denial, siege and battle. Was that really us? Did we spend so many words, waste so much time, use up so much force, forfeit so much happiness? Did we really defend ourselves, instead of surrendering? Unthinkable.

Finally the last vine is picked clean. In the kitchen and hallway we've strung up lines to hang the grapes we've kept in reserve. It's not the same anymore, but it still isn't over. Even now there's something newly ripe. The pomegranates are bursting. There is always more fruit full of juice. The year refuses to end. The fall is still holding its breath. A first, then a second rainstorm comes, huge cloudbursts. Then we sit in the cottage like in an ark, water collects in muddy streams running down the furrows dividing the vine rows, the wind snatches leaves from the vines and trees. We glance at one another, consider our suitcases and build a fire in the hearth. The moisture permeates the bedclothes. I discover a trace of mildew on the wall. Yet, again and again, the sun still takes hold of us. It shines more briefly and less brightly, but we still lie naked in the grass on the lawn, we still swim without shivering.

One day Marianne comes by in a skirt and blouse. I almost don't recognize her. She has become a respectable young woman, a young woman with a last name, and she is seceding from the Saint-Tropez collective.

'I've made up my mind,' she says. 'I leave tomorrow. My bags are already packed. The last two days, rain has been coming down the chimney. My bed is soaked through. Anyway I can't stay here forever, right?'

Marianne says it so off-handedly. But with that, she's broken the spell. All of a sudden it's absolutely and irrevocably fall.

We celebrate her departure. Wolf alternates between ukulele and harmonica. The four of us stroll down to L'Escale. There, too, the season is definitely done. The musicians are gone and the coffee now costs only fifty centimes. The pirate sits alone at his table and looks like he needs a rest. After fornication, hibernation; to everything its season. Only the fishermen's ball obeys no season or calendar. It's as loud and bright as ever. But all of a sudden, we're not in the mood for the din of the orchestrion.

In the early morning it begins to pour, coming down first in fine threads, then thick cords. Saint-Tropez has lost its color: it looks like an old film, scratched and worn and washed out.

We take Marianne to the bus. She kisses us one by one in a line and promises to write. Wolf is wearing a raincoat; he looks like a different person.

Three hours later it's sunny again. After four hours, it's dry. But the spell is broken.

'Wolf,' you say, 'if you like, we can take you with us in the car.'

Wolf gazes at us. Then he says, 'You know, that's exactly what I've been waiting for. I just didn't want to leave this place alone.'

'We leave November first,' you say. 'The day after tomorrow. Don't forget.'

Then you reach across the table to stroke my hand, soothingly, and you say: 'Are you very sad?'

No, I'm not sad. On this score I'm surprised myself, but I can't be sad. Sadness is only for the unfulfilled. It would be an offense against Saint-Tropez to be sad.

I pack our bags. I find a crate filled with wood shavings for our Provençal dishes, which overnight have become souvenirs. An empty grape basket is prepared for Colette. Yes, it's time to go. Summer is behind me; fall too. But not just behind me, also within. In my skin and under my skin.

I know that things are going to get hard now. We'll go back to where we were, under a harsh sky, under a harsh law. Happiness is presumption, and it won't be so lightly pardoned there, even by the gods who give it as a gift. Nor do I know how things will be with you, from now on. We have this, though, at least: a stretch of life shared, a few inches of shared past. Saint-Tropez, the cottage, Colette and the well, the wine harvest and the apricot tree, it all binds us together more tightly than a thousand kisses, or a thousand times in each other's arms.

The next morning we set off. It's a glorious day. Tomorrow is All Souls' Day, but it's hard to believe. I look back once more at the house and the yard. It's like a miracle. November and May melt together. As though this long, unbroken, glowing summer had never been, as though it had not already long been time for nature to draw things to a close, as though here there was simply no exhaustion, no ceasing, no sleep, no decay, everything just as it was on day one: the daisies and roses are opening new flowers, as though they never planned to wilt, and the air is full of butterflies, birds and bees. The geraniums in their earthenware pots have fresh buds. It's warm and blue, and mint and thyme scent the air, the same as always. Time stands still.

I join you and Colette in the car. You try to comfort me.

'We can love each other no matter where,' you say.

But your comfort comes too late; the landscape is there first.

MARION DETJEN

'AT MY DEATH, BURN OR THROW AWAY UNREAD!'

ON THE BACKGROUND OF THE BACKGROUND

Helen Wolff's personal estate is contained in boxes and envelopes in the attic of a small stone house in the mountains of Vermont, close to the sky and in a lovely, self-sufficient solitude that suits her, even if she rarely got to enjoy anything like it in her lifetime. Whenever I come, her son Christian carries the boxes down to the living room and leaves me alone with them for several hours until it is time to eat. In the afternoon, I pull weeds in the garden. Our meals mostly come from there. I can't separate this quiet little house from the material in the boxes, which encompasses an entire century and a vast transatlantic network of connections, yet which is only bound by a single human life, Helen Wolff's life. Nor can I separate my research on Helen's papers from my feelings of gratitude, mixed with a sense of duty, even guilt, for Christian allowing me to invade her private sphere. I am desperately seeking something in this sphere: the truth, the historical truth about our place in the transatlantic twentieth century.

In the summer of 2007, when I was first left alone with Helen's papers, I noticed a thick, rust-brown envelope, torn at the sides, stuffed with manuscripts. On one side, shortly before her death, it would seem, she had written the instruction: 'At my death, <u>burn</u> or throw away <u>unread</u>!' The contents of the envelope were the remains of a literary career Helene* had tried to establish in German, English and—for a time before 1941—French, only to be forced by the circumstances of the time to break off those endeavors. She left behind two finished plays, the novella *Background for Love*, handwritten notes for a longer novel project and at least a dozen essayistic meditations and pieces of documentary non-fiction.

Since founding Pantheon Books in late 1941/early 1942, nine months after fleeing occupied France and arriving in New York, neither Helen Wolff nor her husband Kurt, nor any of the people close to them who knew that she had once wanted to become an author, said a word about these writings. Christian had only stumbled across them in their ominous-looking envelope by accident. My grandmother Liesel, the youngest sister of Aunt Helle, as both her German and her Chilean nieces, nephews, grandnieces and grandnephews called Helen, had given me a shoebox full of letters after Helen's death in 1994 and, with it, the idea of writing a biography. Liesel outlived her older sibling by a decade, but never mentioned Helen's literary efforts. Neither did Kurt Wolff's children from his first marriage—my Uncle Nico and Aunt Maria—nor her younger brother in Chile, Georg, my Uncle Schorsch. The same was obviously true for Helen herself, with whom I had stayed for

---

* Helen Wolff, born as Helene Mosel, adapted her first name to changing surroundings, being called 'Helene' by German-speaking friends even after adopting 'Helen' on her move to the US. Here, I refer to her as 'Helene' when discussing her life before arrival in the US.

several weeks as a young person in 1987–88. At the time I was already trying to discover that thing, that historical truth, which she, as an émigré, a 'witness to the past', a refugee of the lies and schemes of National Socialism, seemed to stand for. How greatly must she and others who experienced the 1930s on the European continent have mistrusted our ability to understand those times? Or did she perhaps just want to spare us? In any case, the knowledge that Helene wanted to become an author and may well have, had the Nazis not come to power, was obviously part of a past that was to be excluded from our memory and had been submerged, along with the rest of ravaged old Europe.

Why didn't she burn or throw away the rust-brown envelope herself? Helen died well prepared and in full possession of her mental powers. As her sole heir, Christian was left to decide whether and how to follow her instruction. Back in 2007, we both felt uncomfortable discussing this issue. At the time, I communicated mainly with his wife Holly, also a passionate historian, about the vagaries of literary judgement that might have led Helen to make this unusual request. Were the texts not good enough to be put in front of readers? Did they not measure up to the exacting standards which Helen maintained as a publisher? The double bind reminded us of Kafka. But was comparing Helen to Kafka itself not a ridiculous sacrilege? Holly and I talked a lot about Uwe Johnson and his obsession with detailed precision. Perhaps that was the real message behind her paradoxical instruction: don't do anything rash with these manuscripts. Be careful, be accurate.

Better not to write or publish anything at all than something ill-considered.

There are obvious, if hardly all-encompassing, reasons why she kept the fruits of her literary labors secret as long as she was a publisher—something she remained for a lucky group of authors until her death. Part of Helen and Kurt Wolff's 'credo' was that the devotion to the books of others demanded by the job of publisher precluded literary activity of one's own. In 1982, when asked why she didn't write any memoirs, she told the *New Yorker*: 'If one writes oneself, one closes out the writing of others. I have never been able to understand editors who could also write. You have to keep yourself open for the creative efforts of authors; you must be totally receptive. It's like being a priest, and I don't think priests should be married.'[1] But even if she was serious about this dubious comparison (her son's best friend was a married minister in New York whom she greatly respected), it didn't explain the secrecy she maintained about her writings at an earlier stage of her life before her career as a publisher.

Perhaps she was afraid of the jealousy and narcissism of the authors with whom she enjoyed such close, almost maternal relationships. Some—Max Frisch, Italo Calvino, Georges Simenon and Uwe Johnson, who dedicated his *Anniversaries* to her—were already dead by the early 1990s. But others— for instance, Günter Grass, Amos Oz, György Konrád and Umberto Eco—outlived her and might have felt overwhelmed by the fact that their ever-attendant publisher and maternal mentor had possessed literary talent of her own. One key element to her success was her ability to take a back seat. She actively silenced attempts to highlight her part in the professional comeback of Kurt, twenty years her senior, who had made a name for himself as the publisher of the Expressionist movement and of Kafka in the 1910s and 1920s.[2] On the other hand, the imprint with which they both continued their work for Harcourt, Brace & World after leaving Pantheon in 1961 named her before her husband. A 'Helen and Kurt Wolff book' was, as Grass noted in his 1994 eulogy for her, like a seal of quality for European literature in the US.[3] And it would retain that status after Kurt Wolff's death in 1963 for the almost three decades during which she ran the imprint as a widow. It was she who tied many of those famous authors to the publishing house, giving them access to the American book market. She acted as their older, maternal friend and advisor, often also on private matters. In her later years she increasingly represented a moral and intellectual authority, as an emigrant of conscience and conviction, and as someone who embodied the best tradition of European literature and European values. At the same time, she possessed the authority of a practical woman, not afraid of hard work, who offered motherly support to authors who had lost their way. She always legitimized her actions by linking them back to Kurt Wolff's legacy. 'I never saw myself in his shadow, I always saw myself in his light,' she invariably answered when asked whether it had been difficult to step out of his shadow after his death.[4] She was highly skeptical of the achievements of the women's liberation movement and often sided with her male authors against feminist attacks by their wives, particularly when the latter claimed to be creative themselves. If her own literary past, with all it entailed, had become known, it would have put her in need of explanation. Perhaps she wanted to spare her prodigy to be in need of explanations in her stead.

When I first read the manuscripts, I would have had a feeling of transgression even without Helen Wolff's paradoxical prohibition—the unsettling sense of viewing something that wasn't meant for my eyes. All of the texts have an autobiographical touch, dealing with private, even intimate subject matter. They work through experiences Helen Wolff obviously had lived through herself, and it's all too easy to decipher which figures correspond to which real-life individuals. The texts remain fictionalized versions of reality and don't allow readers to reconstruct dates, facts and events. But they contain a roman-à-clef level of connection with reality in their depictions of private relationships, their casts and constellations of characters and their settings. Several longer fragments describe Helene's early childhood in the Balkans, first in Serbia, then in Üsküb, which today is Skopje in North Macedonia but which was a provincial capital in the Ottoman Empire until 1912–13. They feature a violent father who's a German businessman and a weak Austrian mother who has almost godlike authority over her children.[5] Both Helene's two plays and her novella *Background for Love* are set in the years before and after the Nazis' rise to power, the time when Kurt and Helen turned their backs—temporarily, then permanently—on Germany. These writings always revolved around an androgynous young woman easily recognizable as Helen herself who, amidst a southern setting, earns her independence so that she can pursue her love of a much older man. They don't directly confront traditional gender roles, but subvert them. The arrangements they reach are anything but conventional, encompassing ménages à trois, polygamy, polyamory and queerness. Invariably, the androgynous woman, not the man, sets the tone. Had these texts been published immediately after Helen's death, without the distancing effect of time passed, questions concerning her biography could easily have become scandals: questions of how Helene Mosel and Kurt Wolff became a couple and a successful husband-and-wife publishing team, or what the story was with her parents; and some of her autobiographical anecdotes quoted in the *New Yorker* would have appeared in a strange light. She didn't want Christian, who had always been very clear about his desire not to get dragged into his parents' affairs, to be confronted with assumptions and speculations. And she probably also wanted to avoid reputational damage to the 'Helen and Kurt Wolff Books' imprint after her death, under her successor Drenka Willen.

The autobiographical background of these texts made it difficult for me to judge their literary quality. For a long time, Christian had no desire to read them. Helen Wolff regarded literature that didn't invent or transform reality in a 'creative' fashion, but rather depicted experiences and the real world as authors found it, as typically feminine, secondary and of lesser value, even if she appreciated other aspects of it. In her eyes, the epitome of such writing were the books of Anne Morrow Lindbergh, whom the Wolffs began publishing with *Gift from the*

Sea in 1955 and with whom they were close friends. Lindbergh wrote unpolitical essays, diaries and letters, and rare works of fiction that were also heavily autobiographical. All her books became bestsellers and represented an important source of income for Pantheon Books, and later Harcourt Brace. Their success was due primarily to their controlled revelation of private observations, experiences and reflections that intersected with the public life of Lindbergh's famous aviator husband Charles. While Charles Lindbergh was the not uncontested American hero, Anne acted as his better, humane and sensitive half, with whom particularly women strongly identified.

Straddling the line between the private and the public required tact and strict observance of proper social form from everyone involved. Anne Morrow Lindbergh had been hounded and traumatized by the media after the kidnapping and murder of her first child in the 1930s. She loved the Wolffs for giving her a 'dignified', discreet publishing avenue. Conversely, Kurt and Helen Wolff credited Lindbergh's works, precisely because of their 'discretion', with a feminine, aesthetical and moral quality which more than compensated for the fact that they were by no means great literature. Helen's stepdaughter in Munich, who translated *Gift from the Sea* and *Dearly Beloved* (1962) into German, joked about the 'crochet work of our dear Anne', whose use of imagery had to be corrected.[6] William Jovanovich, the president of Harcourt Brace, repeatedly stressed how much Lindbergh's manuscripts required Helen Wolff's intensive editing.

If we consider that autobiographical and feminine writing were closely associated and dismissed as non-creative and literarily second-rate, and that the worth of such writing was measured in its tact, noble sentiment and moral refinement, we can perhaps understand why Helen Wolff would prohibit the publication of her own manuscripts. Their literary quality is in fact compromised in some places by an ostentatious confirmation of female subordination that now seems antiquated and can only be explained by Wolff's respect for the standards of her day. Nonetheless, the personality that emerges from these writings has a considerable brash power that is not marked as feminine. In her self-depiction as a child in Üsküb she's something of a hermaphrodite, the best-looking one in the family who prefers to wear trousers and despises and torments her older sister and her worship of princesses. Curly-haired and rosy-cheeked like an angel, the child also walks lamely as though on a devil's club foot—one of her legs was congenitally shorter than the other, giving her a permanent limp. She manipulates all around her, including her mother, and steals food from the pantry with impunity. She's fascinated by a portrait of Napoleon, studying it for hours and deriving strength for the battles she wants to wage in the future. She knows that the protected space her mother has created with her love of higher things, exhortations of tolerance and educational ambitions is fragile, imperiled by the violent unrest in the Balkans, the impending war and, above all, her German father and his savage laughter. The immunity to illusion in a world that is falling apart which this autobiographical protagonist already displays as a child, and her determination to make a way for herself and her talents, also recurs in *Background for Love*, where it subversively inverts and exploits prevailing gender relations. The impoverished, inexperienced young woman takes the French landscape which the experienced, wealthy older man offers her as an alternative vision of life. She radically reinterprets it, changes its meaning and returns it to him in a form that is finally habitable for both of them.

From the very start, Helene Mosel's writing was not a leisure activity. She was under pressure to earn money. Her father had left the family after the First World War and suffered a financial and moral collapse in Constantinople from which he never recovered.[7] Despite many obstacles, her mother had succeeded in getting a good education for their four children. Helene was not able to take her *Abitur*, the qualifying exam for university, but she was admitted as a day student, and the first ever female student, to the prestigious Landheim Schondorf boarding school, where she was considered an exceptionally gifted student with particular linguistic and literary abilities.[8] Thanks to the school, the impecunious young Mosel siblings made contacts that enabled them not only to avoid falling further down the social ladder but ultimately to climb an impressive number of rungs. That rise, however, was anything but easy. Helene Mosel had to work for four years, from 1924 to 1928, as a nanny for a Frankfurt industrialist family.[9] She would later omit this period from all autobiographical statements, as she did with other aspects of her life that could have damaged her reputation as a publisher.

By that point, her mother lived in a shabby attic apartment without a kitchen together with those of Helene's siblings who weren't at boarding schools or otherwise accommodated. When she wasn't suffering from one of her frequent illnesses, she worked as a sales clerk. Her youngest child, my grandmother Liesel, after years of living in foster homes, also briefly attended Schondorf as a ten-year-old, but was expelled for not behaving as was expected of a girl. Shortly before Easter 1924, with things really bad, the eighteen-year-old Helene informed her sick mother that she was trying everything to find money for the family, including selling her own writing. 'Tomorrow, my "Search for Obscurity", the least personal and most consistent of all my literary attempts, is going out to the local newspaper,' she wrote in that letter:

> There's no point, but I don't want to leave any stone unturned. Admittedly, I would have preferred to write only for myself at the start until I found a style of my own. That was the reason for the passivity you accused me of. You seem to have forgotten that I have a job that eats up all my time from morning until 9:30 at night. Then there are letters to write, stockings and linen to stitch, hair to wash, baths, gymnastics and personal hygiene. As a result, I go to bed between 11:30 and midnight. Then I simply *must* read for an hour, until at least 12:30. Where do I have the time and energy to create anything? I'm often surprised that I can scribble together a few pages.[10]

In 1928 the chance materialized, if not to make writing her profession, then at least to work with literature. A maternal friend and mentor, also part of the Schondorf network, introduced her to the Kurt Wolff Publishing House in Munich and

sponsored a three-month internship, giving her the opportunity
to 'make herself indispensable'. Helene's greatest asset was her
multilingualism, which earned her translation assignments.
Already in decline by this point, the publishing house was a
far cry from what it had been in the 1910s, when it was the
outlet for the new generation of young Expressionist writers.[11]
It only published ten books in 1928, the majority about art,
two for gourmets and a novel by Joseph Roth. Almost all its
major authors had left, often under unpleasant circumstances.
Kurt Wolff managed to maintain friendships with a few, chiefly
Walter Hasenclever, René Schickele and Franz Werfel. Joseph
Roth only stayed because he could extract the highest possible
royalties from Kurt Wolff.[12] Having been located since 1919 in
a luxurious Italian Baroque villa on Königsplatz, at that point
the publishing house was little more than a forum for Wolff
and his first wife's high-society activities. Elisabeth Wolff came
from the venerable industrial Merck family, a wealthy clan very
mindful of tradition, who combined business acumen with
consciousness of their social class and an extremely rarefied
taste in art. Duchess Mechtilde Lichnowsky, née Countess
von und zu Arco-Zinneberg, French envoy Count Charles
François de Paule Lefèvre d'Ormesson, the antique bookseller
and literary historian Curt von Faber du Faur and various art
history professors, art collectors and art dealers were among
the Wolffs' circle. Kurt Wolff possessed great charm, was very
popular with women, and was not averse to the odd clandestine
affair. Female employees loyal to him mostly ran the everyday
business of the publishing house in those days.[13]

Kurt Wolff's publishing focus at that time had shifted outside Germany. Like Roth, Hasenclever, Kurt Tucholsky and others, Wolff had mentally and emotionally distanced himself from Germany already after the failure of the 1919 revolution, and ostentatiously turned toward European and non-European literature, art and art history in 1924. Encouraged by advances in printing technology, he had co-founded a new publishing house for art, Pantheon Casa Editrice in Florence, which was conceived as thoroughly European and international. It commissioned the most respected art historians in Europe to write overviews of certain epochs and genres for an educated but not academic public. They appeared simultaneously in translation in Germany, Italy, France, Spain, Britain and the US. Each book contained up to a hundred illustrations prepared for all editions in a single print run, often printed by hand by the Officina Bodoni art press, which belonged to Wolff's friend Hans Mardersteig, in Verona. These extremely elaborate works targeted a small audience of wealthy American and European art lovers, who bought the books on the basis of individual subscriptions. Central to the publishers' ethos was the attempt to break through national boundaries in understanding art. Individual volumes discussed Italian painting, German sculpture or French engravings, but these were always treated as transnational intersections, never in isolation. A book about Islamic architecture also showed that the publishers conceived of European art as open to global ideas of culture.

The Pantheon Casa Editrice was an endeavor close to Wolff's heart, and he devoted the lion's share of his time, energy and financial resources to it. But ultimately he was overwhelmed by the project's ambitions. As Wolff was refocusing further in the direction of Europeanization and globalization, European society was headed backwards. The nationalism that spread throughout the continent in the late 1920s reduced the potential audience for transnational art books to a tiny, barely perceivable niche, and currency and customs hurdles that accompanied the return of many nationalist restrictions robbed the Pantheon Casa Editrice of much of its *raison d'être*.

The perils of Wolff's transnational enterprise are illustrated by the story of his primary partner, John Holroyd Reece. Reece was a purportedly English art book dealer and publisher in Paris, who employed Helene Mosel on various occasions in the 1930s. Along with Wolff, he was the principal owner of Pantheon Casa Editrice and was responsible for the production and distribution of the books in English and French. Although only thirty years old, he enjoyed major business success while Wolff continually lost money after the German hyperinflation of 1923 and was forced in 1926 to auction off his private collection of rare fifteenth- and sixteenth-century incunables to prop up his share of Pantheon. Tensions crept into the two men's relationship, and quarrels were frequent. In the summer of 1930 Wolff, with the help of a private detective and lots of expensive research, carried out by Helene among others, discovered that he had been conned. Reece's real name was Riess, and he was actually the son of a Bavarian rabbi who had been sent to an elite British public school when he was a teenager. An older, wealthy friend of the family had paid for his education and taught him to speak upper-class British English. Claiming to be from the highest echelons of British society and to have studied at Cambridge, the highly intelligent, multilingual Reece had been able to make the sort of business connections in Paris that classism and anti-Semitism would otherwise have denied the son of a broken Jewish home from the Bavarian provinces.[14]

Reece's circumstances, which explain a certain ruthlessness in his business dealings, were unknown in 1928, when Helene started working for Kurt Wolff in Munich, but formed the backdrop against which her new employer was operating. In a flurry of desperate activity, Wolff devoted himself to Pantheon, his 'beloved problem child', neglecting the publishing house that bore his name and its subsidiaries.[15] Increasingly, their main business consisted of selling off rights and stock to other publishers and searching for funds to stave off imminent bankruptcy. As the Kurt Wolff Publishing House shrank and its employees were let go, Kurt Wolff's activities in Italy and France opened up a special position and future career prospects for Helene—as a diligent, multilingual translator who could also take care of correspondence, draw up indices and edit texts. However, she still lived on a meager salary in the attic apartment with her mother, her sister and two subletters, working herself to the brink of exhaustion, often going without enough to eat.[16]

Shortly before moving to Munich, Helene had gotten engaged to Alfred von Beckerath, a composer and musician whose financial situation was scarcely better than her own. Nonetheless, despite his own lack of work, 'Alfi' or 'Alf', as he was known, supported her family as best he could. He was well liked but not taken very seriously by the Mosels, who always tried to see the humor in their difficulties. While Helene's father lived off his new wife in the poorest of circumstances in Berlin and repeatedly sent ever nastier blackmail letters to Munich, her mother and elder sister Ena pinned their hopes on finding husbands who would at least offer a measure of financial security. Ena, in particular, had a talent for converting her erotic adventures and misadventures into 'the most delightful cinema'. Helene laughed at these performances but considered her mother and sister's capitulation in the face of material necessity undignified, insisting on earning her keep herself.

In the rust-brown envelope there is an undated text, probably written in the early 1930s, that bears the title 'Praise for Poverty'. It's a hymn to impoverishment as a necessary, justified, God-given test to be passed. This may have been partly a romanticization. When Helene wrote the text, the worst of her money problems were behind her. But she clearly valued the experience of doing without possessions. Under no circumstances, she claimed, would she have wanted to trade places with blithely privileged ladies like Wolff's wife Elisabeth. Not only this text, but all of Helene's surviving letters from after 1929 reveal a pronounced, conscious conviction that the social circumstances at the root of wealth and poverty were outdated and that they harmed also the privileged few by robbing them of opportunities for personal development. Helene's 'Praise for Poverty' contained a certain snobbishness toward the 'Munich lifestyle and everything connected to it', which included the

Wolff household, along with a description of the inner lack of freedom and the intellectual and spiritual dead end to which that lifestyle ostensibly led.[17]

In fact, in the late 1920s the Wolffs weren't in a very good state at all. The once and future slender and elegant grand seigneur had grown bloated and overweight from too much food and drink. His diary depicts him as restless, frenetic and prone to stay away from home, attending lectures, accepting invitations and visiting friends. To save the Pantheon Casa Editrice and avoid losing more of his private wealth, Wolff hoped he could attract the support of a patron from the world of American high finance. His would-be savior, however, was hesitant. Thus in early 1929 he wrote that he had 'arrived at the conclusion that I will have to take a passive, wait-and-see stance until at least the fall'. He added, 'I find maintaining this passivity almost paralytically strenuous, infinitely more difficult than some form of clearly defined activity.'[18] With her marriage disintegrating, Elisabeth Wolff sought healing and spiritual solace in Christian Science. The couple's son Nikolaus would recall her dragging him to readings of Mary Baker Eddy's writings every Sunday in Munich's Tonhalle auditorium.[19] In March 1929 Elisabeth, five months pregnant, suffered a miscarriage and fell seriously ill. She had to spend several weeks in the hospital, where she fell in love with the Red Cross clinic's director and gynecologist Hans Albrecht, whom she would marry after divorcing Kurt Wolff. Nevertheless, from the outside the couple's life seemed unchanged. Kurt visited Elisabeth in hospital at least once every day, and they later undertook joint trips and excursions.

Their marriage was dissolved without haste, by consensus and in a friendly manner.

We don't know when Kurt Wolff and Helene Mosel became a couple. In November 1928 she accompanied him to Paris for two weeks. That was a 'huge honor' according to her mother, who despite her affection for 'good-hearted Alfi' had nothing at all against her daughter's budding love affair with the publisher.[20] In the wake of the trip, Helene was commissioned for her first major translation from French: *Romanesque Sculpture in Eleventh- and Twelfth-Century France*, a badly written, unedited art history manuscript by Paul Deschamps. She worked 'like an obsessive'[21] into the summer on her 'damn Deschamps',[22] going without sleep and food and neglecting her health. Her family helped, drawing up vocabulary lists, typing, and staying in the apartment, so that Kurt Wolff could reach her whenever he wanted. When she was finished, her reward was 100 marks and a raise to a salary of 200 marks, the same as long-term female Kurt Wolff Verlag employees received. In early July 1929 she got to see more of the world as Kurt Wolff's private secretary. She was summoned to Zürich, where she met Elisabeth and lived with the couple, who had already decided to separate, in the Hotel Dolder. For a week she was 'quite spoiled' and 'thoroughly fattened up'.[23]

Although Alf von Beckerath had gotten a job in Wiesbaden in the meantime, Helene's mother didn't object when Wolff and her daughter made plans that September for another trip that was business in name only. They would travel alone for six weeks to a hotel in Menton, a coastal town on the French

Riviera near the Italian border. They drove there together in Wolff's large Buick.[24] His diary recorded the details of the trip. At 5 a.m. on 13th September they set out and drove to Grenoble via Lindau, Zürich, Aarau, Solothurn, Neuchâtel, Lausanne and Geneva. The next day they pressed on to Nice, where they spent two nights. On the 16th they took up their vacation residence in the Hôtel des Anglais in Menton. There are no entries for the days that followed. In early October they were paid a visit by a Pantheon Casa Editrice employee from Paris, and Walter Hasenclever also visited in mid-October. On 26th October they started their return journey at 4 a.m., driving through Avignon, Antibes, Cannes, Aix, Arles and Nîmes. The next day took them via Orange and Montélimar to Lyons, and on the 28th they arrived in Paris, where they spent a little less than a week. On 2nd November they returned via Augsburg to Munich. By the time they got to Paris, sharing a hotel room was no longer possible. Helene stayed with a co-worker, and Kurt Wolff with John Holroyd Reece. The affection and time they had shared together gave her no claim on a permanent relationship. A year later, Helene still called the trip 'an opportune minute under opportune skies for a fleeting dalliance'.[25]

Obviously these weeks in southern France, together with two other summers—1931 and 1932—which the couple spent in the south of France, were the real-life inspiration for the story in *Background for Love*. The encounter with Hasenclever and probably the visit to the casino took place during the first trip in 1929. In the novella, Hasenclever is a small fellow named Erich, a 'lively little marmoset, soft and good-hearted' who convinces the female narrator to get off the train, scribbling down the names of places on a scrap of paper: 'Saint-Raphaël and Toulon, Le Lavandou you can't miss, he grows enthusiastic, makes me eager as well'. Erich knows southern France just as well as the narrator's lover and has a much better sense of what will be good for her.

Today Hasenclever is known, if at all, as an early Expressionist. But by the 1920s both he and Kurt Wolff had distanced themselves from that movement. Hasenclever was among the German writers and journalists who had made France their adopted country and supported German-French dialogue, in contrast to the hatred and contempt the majority of German society felt toward the French 'arch-enemy' for the Treaty of Versailles, the seizure of Alsace-Lorraine and especially the 1923 occupation of the Ruhr region. Many of Kurt Wolff's former authors took part in this discussion: not just politically active writers like Heinrich Mann, Ernst Toller and Walter Mehring, but also those who had entirely given up on politics like René Schickele, Annette Kolb and Hasenclever himself. On the French side, they had partners who also propagated good relations between the countries: André Gide, Jules Romains, the German literature scholar Félix Bertaux and, most notably, Nobel Prize laureate and Kurt Wolff author Romain Rolland, who was considered a major Germanophile. The French-German foreign policy rapprochement under the two foreign ministers Aristide Briand and Gustav Stresemann helped to intensify and institutionalize the exchange between writers and intellectuals. As of 1924, many German authors reported as culture correspondents in Paris for progressive German newspapers: Hasenclever for Berlin's *8 Uhr-Abendblatt*, Rudolf Leonhard and Kurt Tucholsky for the *Weltbühne* and the *Vossische Zeitung*, and also Siegfried Kracauer, Ernst Toller and Joseph Roth at different times for various papers.

In Paris, Hasenclever became good friends with Tucholsky, who returned to Berlin in 1926 to become editor-in-chief of the *Weltbühne*. The two men later intermittently shared an apartment and wrote plays together. Another close acquaintance of Hasenclever's was the Paris correspondent for the *Frankfurter Zeitung*, Friedrich Sieburg. They all presented France to their German readers as a place to be longed for, more attractive than Germany: with great wine and food, beautiful women, high aesthetic sensibility, greater appreciation of individuality and freedom, and a more humane way of life. Nonetheless, behind their Francophilia they maintained completely contradictory, indeed mutually exclusive ideas. For Hasenclever and Heinrich Mann, who gave a lecture in Paris in 1928 on the 'intellectual Locarno', France embodied the principles of 1789: *liberté, égalité, fraternité*, the tradition of Enlightenment and self-emancipation, with which—at least it was hoped—communists, socialists and the liberal bourgeois could all identify. But by no means did all Francophiles agree with Mann's emphasis on France's universal humanist, revolutionary tradition.

In 1929, the year of Helene's first trip with Kurt Wolf, Sieburg published a very successful book entitled *God in France? An Attempted Explanation*. It focused not on the country as the birthplace of the republican ideals of 1789 but on the religious nationalism with which Jeanne d'Arc had once united the French people. 'Every path to the core of the French being starts with Jeanne d'Arc,' wrote Sieburg.[26] He proposed that France had a basic 'faith', a religiously anchored cultural structure that made it a nation of continuity, reason, civilization and moderation—and thus also a bulwark against untethered modernity, capitalism and consumerism. The authentic French experience, he claimed, was to peacefully and without coercion or exploitation tend their gardens, fields and vineyards, cultivating nature, and then enjoy red wine and white bread after work with their families. All of these topoi can also be found in *Background for Love*. However, in contrast to Helene, Sieburg felt indivisibly bound to the 'German people', which added a pronounced, ultimately fatal note of resentment to his admiration of the French. In his eyes, the life of the Germans was quite sad and grim since they didn't define themselves culturally but ethnically and only ever produced solitary genius isolated from the militant, anti-intellectual masses, whereas in France intellectuals were integrated as a matter of course into society. But the future belonged to the Germans. France was 'finished', at the end of its development, and 'mentally besieged' by the inevitable, new, violent creativity represented by Germany. It would be entirely possible for the Germans to sideline obdurate, idiosyncratic France and ignore it politically. But that would have been akin to the Germans shunting all the 'holy qualities' of the French—white bread and red wine, joie de vivre, the heavenly calm, the simple sense of proportion and indeed the whole idea of civilization—on to an 'Indian reservation' and revealing themselves to be barbarians. Instead, Sieburg argued, Germany could use these qualities to ennoble their triumphant progress. Thus Sieburg's bestseller was only superficially a declaration of love for France. In fact, it was an insult and a declaration of war, fed by a mixture of German megalomania and inferiority complex. France should serve to prevent Germany from becoming like the USA, his bête noire, the likewise modern and vital, but capitalist and soulless America. It offered him a temporary respite 'because I want to catch my breath and linger for a while before the wave [of modernity] rips me from the old world and plunges me into that destiny which transforms me from a connoisseur to a consumer' and 'because I'm weak enough to prefer to exist in an old-fashioned, disorderly paradise than in an antiseptic and bleak exemplary world'. It is no great surprise, then, that Sieburg, who continued to work as a Paris correspondent for the *Frankfurter Zeitung* after 1933, later supported the Nazi regime and made a career under the Third Reich as a red-wine-drinking embassy press advisor in occupied France. He was part of the project to integrate 'sweet old France' into Adolf Hitler's 'new Europe'.

In the fateful years following 1929, the German nationalist back door which Sieburg left open in his ostensible homage to France was quietly but decidedly closed upon Helene, Hasenclever and others. Helene, too, saw an irreconcilable contradiction between Germany and France, but one of inim-ical principles, not nations. The conflict was between a 'cold, severe, rules-obsessed' world, prone to creating borders and hostile to the good life, and a warm, life-affirming world that overcame borders and embraced all of humanity. 'Maybe there is no such thing as a fatherland, as they call it back home', she wrote in her novel, 'and borders are arbitrary and that's why they're so often moved around, here as there; what there are instead are climates, milder and harsher, rougher and gentler, and climates kind to us humans.' The principles represented by Germany and France collided in heaven, in the realm of belief, emotion and thought, not on earth and in politics. The German principle treated political boundaries as boundaries of world view. The French principle was to overcome political boundaries and to make viewing the world a personal responsibility. The narrator of *Background for Love* has completely internalized the French principle and vows never to lose it, no matter the political circumstances. Walter Benjamin would have criticized this avoidance of politics as an outmoded bourgeois habit of shutting oneself off from the world. But Helene no longer ran the risk of falling into the nationalist trap of 'my country, right or wrong' which led so many of her formerly liberal, bourgeois contemporaries to support the Nazi dictatorship in the end.

The six weeks from mid-September to late October 1929 which Helene, Kurt Wolff and Hasenclever spent in southern France witnessed several events on the German, European and world political stages that directly affected them. On 3rd October, Germany's foreign minister, Gustav Stresemann, died, heralding the end of the policies of Franco-German and European understanding that had been a precondition for the international ethos behind Pantheon Casa Editrice. And the crash on Wall Street and the start of the Great Depression in late October killed off any hope of Pantheon's being rescued by cash injections from an American patron. The stock market crash also rocked Helene's private circles. Many of the Frankfurt families who had at times supported the Mosels suddenly faced 'grave worries'. In the weeks after the crash, Alfred von Beckerath had to deal not only with Helene's termination of their relationship and engagement but with the loss of the final remnants of his parents' wealth too.

By the end of 1929, Kurt Wolff's various publishing houses ceased production of new books. He tried, wherever possible, to sell their stock, especially the renowned and expensively produced art volumes, to other publishers and to bookshops. Wolff's shares in Patheon Casa Editrice ended up over the course of the following months in the hands of John Holroyd Reece. Helene was involved in the entire clean-out while simultaneously translating a book about sixteenth- and seventeenth-century British painting from English to German for Pantheon. Her romantic relationship with Wolff still had to be kept strictly under wraps. The only one who knew about their affair was Annemarie von Puttkamer, Wolff's ex-lover and mother of his out-of-wedlock son. She served as a deliverer of messages, letters and bouquets of flowers, and sometimes the three of them attended the theater together. At this point, Helene had to finance both her mother and Ena, who was unable to find work, which often caused quarrels between the two sisters. Her brother also could barely subsist on the pittance he earned as an apprentice at IG Farben in Frankfurt. To help her family, Helene repeatedly accepted money from Wolff, although she found it 'rather embarrassing'.[27] She had no claim to a permanent relationship with him so she had to content herself with 'the moment', 'the preciously gifted minute' and the 'torn, furtive scraps of time in which every word tumbles from my heart because I know that in two minutes the car will stop on the corner, and it will be over'.[28] There was only one way to continue her career and save her love: leave Munich and continue working for Pantheon, although no longer as an employee of Wolff, but rather of Reece and Pegasus Press.

The idea to do this seems to have arisen in early December 1929 during a visit by Reece to Munich. In the middle of that month, Helene was making preparations for Wolff to attend a general Pantheon meeting in Florence. The following February, draft contracts were exchanged.[29] As she put it, her move to Paris 'weighed on her soul like a mountain' since she had no assurance that her relationship with Wolff would survive spatial separation at a point when 'very many aspects of it appeared dubious, problematic and uncertain concerning genuineness and duration'.[30] Nonetheless, she saw such separation as a necessity for her to have a lasting relationship with him in the first place. 'Sometimes I think that the beginning of our relations still lies in the distant future, as though I, and he as well, still have a lot more to experience and must become much more adult. Therefore, I don't shudder at the thought of Paris. On the contrary, for reasons of self-preservation, it's necessary for us to separate so that I do not revolve [around him] as a smaller planet does a larger one, but instead, alone, and in the most profound sense alone, become a human being… in order to then encounter one another again.'[31]

Indeed, Kurt Wolff still had a long way to go before he would be able to break his 'Munich bonds'. He continued to live a life, albeit less opulent, of social receptions, teas, visits and excursions, and outsiders still considered him Elisabeth's husband. He traveled with her to Berlin and Leipzig and spent the Christmas holidays and occasional evenings with her and their children. At the same time, the two were pushing ahead with their divorce, and Elisabeth spent time at the home of her future husband, Hans Albrecht, while Wolff was together with Helene. The heated atmosphere of anti-Semitism, nationalism and popular resentment during the Great Depression and the rise of Nazism—Munich was considered the 'capital of the [Nazi] movement'—also colored the congregations of art lovers, bibliophiles and professors with whom Wolff socialized in the winter of 1929–30.[32]

One focal point of conservative attention in the networks in which Wolff moved was the poet Stefan George. Wolff greatly admired George as a poet, but he had long turned his back on George's ideas of a 'new empire' (*neues Reich*) and the entire quasi-philosophical claptrap and elitist, esoteric posturing of the George circle.[33] Responding to her brother, who sought happiness in the George cult after graduating from high school in 1929, Helene mocked the pseudo-faith in the 'George-style cross of Apollo and Baldur'.[34] She wrote to Liesel that she 'did not want to say anything about George, because I am admittedly of two minds': 'The actual George with his fetish for men's clubs is deeply alien to my very core. I find a few of his poems very formally beautiful, others, for their content, unsettling, prophetic and of a stature that cannot be denied.'[35] In 1934, while in French exile, Helene wrote of Kurt Wolff being still 'entirely besotted with George's poetry' (*ganz vergeorgt*).[36] And in New York, one of the first books his newly founded publishing house would bring out was a lovingly prepared bilingual German-English George anthology.

Wolff and Helene simply ignored other conservative intellectual focal points like Ernst Jünger or Carl Schmitt. Nevertheless, their personal tastes notwithstanding, Wolff's connections, memberships and social set in the final years of the Weimar Republic involuntarily put him in the right-wing, nationalist, anti-democratic political camp. Up to a certain point he tried to adapt to the renationalization and to the right-wing shift in an attempt to save the international company Pantheon Casa Editrice. He was a member of the European Cultural Association, founded by the Austrian Prince Karl Anton Rohan, which sought to bring together the 'intellectual elite' in a cross-border cultural network.[37] Every year, members met for congresses in various European cities, and national chapters organized talks by foreign guests. Initially, Rohan pitched his efforts to promote cross-European understanding as apolitical and pluralistic, but from the very start he pitted 'the ideas of 1914' against the 'ideas of 1789' and Western rationalism, rejecting the League of Nations and any visions of a federal Europe. In his eyes, elites were tasked with building 'bridges between peoples' without those peoples losing their autonomous national cultures.[38] By the early 1930s, the Cultural Association had grown so close to fascism and revolutionary nationalism that even men like Hermann Göring and Nazi ideologue Alfred Rosenberg began taking an interest. For Wolff the Association was primarily a network for soliciting useful contacts and support for Pantheon's expensively produced art volumes. If he wanted to continue profiting from his membership of the 'elite', with its wealth and influence, he would have to accept that his apolitical, transnational projects would get sucked into the centrifugal force of Nazism.

Thus it wasn't just financial concerns, but the entire highly contradictory, nigh on insoluble situation that put Wolff under extreme pressure and made him decide to sell off all his publishing shares, including those in Pantheon Casa Editrice, in the spring of 1930. With that, he liquidated his existence as a publisher and a leading Munich personality. He had no plan B and no professional prospects. With vastly diminished private assets, he faced a completely uncertain future.

Without Helene, it's unlikely that Wolff would have summoned the inner strength for this drastic step and the accompanying arduous, time-consuming clean-up and 'liquidation work, which was as horrible as it was well deserved'.[39] Helene had already set off for Paris on 9th April 1930 and was working in the offices of the Pegasus Press, but she was still paid by Wolff and provisionally quartered with another Pantheon employee named Helene Wünsche. The letters that Wolff sent her that month—hastily composed, brief but almost desperately tender and loving missives—evince the importance he attached to changing and liberating himself from his contradictory bonds and entanglements. He longed to free himself, he wrote, from 'all this undergrowth, in a fashion right and proper', to shed 'all this weight and all these burdens' and be 'praised' by the woman he now called 'you darling, lightly hovering creature'. Poor, single and unattached, Helene had the qualities needed to correctly judge Kurt Wolff's situation, but she apparently also felt inhibited by his status, once admitting that it was difficult for her to express herself freely toward him. He promised to give her the 'possibility' of doing so, although he conceded that in his present circumstances he felt unable to give up his 'unrest', 'paralyzing exhaustion' and 'drinking bouts'. He added: 'Please think over what I need to do and become so that you can also speak with me, face to face, my darling, darling girl Helene. I so desire to become as you deem fit.—That will certainly be right. It is also certain that I will leave Munich in May. Believe me: many things will get better. I know that you have patience. Don't lose it. Most likely I won't drink and will eat little for a while. I feel very acutely how good, beneficial and necessary that will be. No doubt I will also be able to *love* you in a better, stronger and more upstanding way.'[40]

One very painful consequence of liquidating the Kurt Wolff Verlag was that in doing so he put Annemarie von Puttkamer in a precarious position. She still served as the conduit for all letters and contact between Kurt and Helene. Wolff once wrote that he loved Helene 'mutually' with Annemarie, a term that left open whether he loved both women or whether he and Annemarie loved Helene. In any case, Annemarie was as deeply involved in Kurt and Helene's love affair as Helene was in Kurt's concern for Annemarie and their son Enoch. Nicknamed 'Plum', the child had fallen seriously ill and was unable to remain with the foster family who had raised him thus far. Wolff cared for Annemarie and offered advice, but he never assumed full responsibility as a father. As the day approached when the small boy would have to be picked up from his foster parents, a journey that loomed before Annemarie 'like a nightmare', Wolff asked Helene to come back from Paris and accompany her.[41] It was beyond discussion that Wolff, as the boy's biological father, should escort Annemarie or provide him with a home and upkeep. Enoch didn't even know who his father was at the time.

So it was that Helene only stayed three weeks in Paris, before returning to Munich in early May for a few weeks to help Kurt Wolff sort out his personal affairs. The agreement was that she would return to work at Pegasus on 1st July—this time in the employ of Reece, not Wolff. A letter from her mother to her brother Georg spells out how precarious the family's situation was. 'If everything goes belly up, which I hope doesn't happen,' wrote her mother, at least she could go to Alf in Berlin, 'although admittedly he couldn't pay her a salary'.[42] Wolff's calendar indicates that he was reunited with Helene on 2nd May and that the following day the two had lunch with Annemarie and Enoch 'downstairs' on Königinstrasse and that they dined 'upstairs' in the evening with Elisabeth and Annemarie. It's impossible to ascertain whether Helene went with Annemarie to pick up her son. But according to a letter written by her sister ten days later, she had been forced to go on a solitary vacation to a rural estate in Pomerania where, following the long, arduous journey to northern Germany, she seemed 'to be bored to death, for which she had her beloved Kurt to thank since he had given her this burden'.[43] This makes it likely that she had to bring poor Enoch to his new home, either alone or together with Annemarie. The estate was the ancestral home of the noble Puttkamer dynasty.

Meanwhile, Wolff traveled to Lake Geneva to personally explain the demise of his publishing house to Romain Rolland. On 16th May 1930 he departed Munich for an indefinite time, taking his cello and the correspondence he needed to attend to. He checked into a spa, the sanatorium in Fürstenberg Castle on the Havel River, also in the north of Germany. It was run by a friend, the neurologist Dr Viktor Emil von Gebsattel, whose wife, 'the amiable Karoline', Wolff got along particularly well with.[44] Helene and Annemarie joined him a week later. After two days Annemarie traveled on, but Helene stayed. As far as the others knew, she was Wolff's private secretary. She wrote to her brother Georg that she worked for around four hours a day while Kurt, who finally 'has run away from the domestic hearth', devoted himself to his recovery. 'The human factor is exhausting—Kurt has after all reached a point at which others suffer nervous breakdowns. He's restless, nervous and indecisive. Actually, there can be no talk of recovery. The only thing you can do is stay calm yourself, keep your nerves and balance out the atmosphere with your own natural self-control.

Believe me: That's not always easy.'[45] On the other hand, the physical setting where Helene had to perform her balancing act couldn't have been any lovelier: a Baroque riverside castle in a lake district in summer. It was hardly the worst place to spend time.

Still, the uncertain future and the sudden separation from the sphere of influential, famous and important people must have weighed heavily on Kurt Wolff. Very few voices from his former life reached him in the sanatorium: a sympathy card from Romain Rolland and a very understanding, lengthy letter from Franz Werfel, who paid tribute to the Kurt Wolff Verlag as 'the literary instrument of the last poetic movement that has existed in Germany'. He also predicted that great things lay in store for Wolff himself, even if the generation of 1914 and the First World War, which had coalesced in the publishing house and to which Werfel himself belonged, was forgotten and silent.[46]

In late June, Helene left Fürstenberg and Wolff to return to work in Paris, but he didn't have to make do without female companionship. Annemarie took Helene's place, and then a week later Helene Wünsche, and Karoline stayed there the entire time. Moreover, Kurt and Helene arranged several occasions when they could meet in beautiful, interesting places and be together. In July, on her birthday, Wolff invited her to London for three days. Her brother was the only one whom she told about these rendezvous—in letters she instructed him to destroy. Three weeks later, she went to the French coastal town of Saint-Malo and was taken by steamship to the island of Jersey, where she covertly spent eight days with Wolff—'probably the most heavenly of my existence thus far'.[47] For the first time they were alone with one another, not in a luxurious, socially elevated environment but in a simple farmhouse. 'You know, it seems to me', she wrote to Georg, 'that to lead a simple life for once with K., with no people, only nature, a gentle, lovely, cheery cove, to be able to swim, take walks, converse and be silent a lot—if under such circumstances, a man loves you more than ever, then it's no longer whimsy and dalliance.' Indeed, throughout that summer and the following winter Wolff concentrated on thinning out the 'undergrowth' of his previous bonds and simplifying his life as best he could. Having weighed eighty-three kilograms in Munich, he trimmed down to seventy-seven in late August and sixty-eight by the end of the year—what he considered his ideal weight, which he would maintain from then on. Helene grew increasingly confident that their relationship would last, was hardly able to comprehend 'a man capable of such love' and rhapsodized about Wolff's 'beauty and nobility in expression and bearing, this captivating mixture of intellect and soul'. She wrote: 'Georg, it is better to spend a week per year with such a person and the rest alone than to compromise and never be alone throughout the year... You don't have to want to possess what you love. You have to truly love it in order to know one another and to be indestructibly bound by the strength of feeling: then there is no distance and no jealousy and no resentment.'[48]

In Paris Helene lived for the first time in an apartment of her own, located on Boulevard Saint-Michel: 'I have a tiny apartment, a little front room with a gas oven, a built-in cupboard and a sink, where I can cook and do the washing,' she wrote to Georg:

> The WC with no W, very primitive, and a room that's like a cell, only with tulle blinds before the windows, no curtains, carpet, etc. A bed, a fireplace, a chair, a table, another chair—that's it. My overturned steamer trunk is on one wall, shamefacedly veiled. My books, photos, etc. are on top of it. As the room is small, it's better empty than full. My life in it runs like this: 2x a week a man (men are easier to find here than women) sweeps the floor, polishes the aluminum silverware and brass things, i.e. the basic cleaning. I cram everything else—the bed, the washing, the cooking, washing the dishes and my hosiery, and darning my clothes—into the hours before between and after work. I always cook for myself. It's so much cheaper. I also do my own shopping, 2x a week at the market that's thankfully located close to the office. That's how I spend my free time, and it eats up lots of it.[49]

It's surprising that she was able to afford a cleaner twice a week. Was domestic help so cheap—and those who did it so impoverished—that even people of little visible means like Helene with her meager wage could afford their services? In the same letter that she wrote about her cleaner, Helene thanked her brother for sending her money he had scraped together by going hungry, so that she could purchase something to wear. After their week in Jersey, Kurt Wolff spent three days incognito with Helene in Paris and took the opportunity to furnish her apartment with curtains, books, faience and other nice things.

There was a lot to do in the office, and the atmosphere was tense since Pantheon was doing 'very badly under the new management' and Reece and Wolff had broken ties, the latter owing the former money. Secretly, Wolff and Helene went to great lengths to procure evidence that Reece came from a poor Jewish-German family and not from the English upper classes—evidence that would have been perfect for an attempt at blackmail. It seems, though, that Kurt Wolff didn't use this material against Reece, instead keeping it and taking it with him to America, where today it remains a bizarre element in the literary estate of Helen and Kurt Wolff at Yale University.

The conflict between Wolff and Reece put Helene in an impossible position. Reece was oblivious to their relationship, and she depended upon him for her livelihood. On the other hand, her loyalties resided with Wolff, and it seemed but a matter of time until he would have to maintain her, if their affair was to continue. The summer passed, and fall arrived, and Kurt continued to lead an unsettled existence between Fürstenberg, Munich and various places abroad, while Helene performed her daily balancing act with Reece in the Paris office. Again, her brother Georg was the only person she felt she could tell that she suffered from insomnia and loss of appetite, that she frequently felt ill and that her neither-here-nor-there situation was 'more than embarrassing'.[50]

During this period, Helene read an essay which left her 'very enthusiastic' and about which she wrote to her brother. Entitled

'Possibilities and Limits of Community', it appeared in 1930 in a rather obscure journal to which Alf likely alerted her. It formulated the basic metaphysical and ethical underpinning that would inform Helene's views and beliefs in the decades to come.[51] The author was Romano Guardini, a Catholic theologian who occupied a chair in religious philosophy and Catholicism and who created a stir with his ideas on how to renew the Catholic faith, which had spread from France to Germany at the beginning of the twentieth century. The starting point for Guardini's considerations was the great dream of human solidarity, felt by many early-twentieth-century young people, who discovered that they could speak in terms of 'we' and throw open the 'doors of the ego', so that 'the terrible and selfish individualism of the day could be overcome and community became possible'.[52] The disappointment to which this discovery had been exposed since then, Guardini proposed, could only be countered with a 'personally and ethically worked-out world view', in which every individual formed his or her own 'personal center' in his or her direct relationship with God. Overlapping 'ancillary worlds… with their special interpretations, evaluations and teleologies' grouped themselves around these centers. In this polycentric view, love, relationships, self-fulfillment and the overcoming of loneliness and egotism could be achieved through 'personal behavior' insofar as people attempted in constant, fundamental motion to reach the personal core of others. Guardini called this 'being-in-motion toward the you'.[53]

Guardini wasn't the only philosopher Helene read. She constantly had volumes by better-known figures, especially

Schopenhauer and Montaigne, by her side. But as much as Schopenhauer's misanthropy and Montaigne's skepticism may have appealed to her cosmopolitan cleverness and her clear-eyed view of how her contemporaries were mauling one another in a general European civil war, the decisions and actions she took in concrete situations can be related back most directly to Catholic personalism. For her, the uncertainties, asymmetries and external dependencies in her relationship with Wolff were not only tolerable. They spurred her on to further self-development, to 'being-in-motion toward the you', as long as she and Kurt maintained a dialogue in their stolen moments together and as long as he showed himself to be 'a person capable and ready for change, thoroughly lively, and not hidden behind a mask'. She wrote to Georg: 'One thing I do know. Whatever may become of my relationship, and it can mean endless difficulty and suffering, it was necessary, indeed unavoidable. And now it is as it is. If he comes, it's wonderful. If he doesn't come, it's good too. The most wonderful thing is and remains that he wants to return and see me again precisely *because* I never talk about him returning and us seeing one another again. That's the way life seems to me: what a human being *doesn't need* is what he should have. (I mean this metaphysically—one shouldn't be required to have anything.)'[54]

At the time, Georg was undergoing a severe personal crisis, feeling himself unable to square his idealistic desires and ambitions with the narrow confines and constraints of his material existence as an apprentice at IG Farben in Frankfurt. Helene wrote him long letters in which she drew parallels between his life and hers and offered philosophical advice. 'As in the fairy tale, you have to eat through a wall of rice pudding before you arrive at the land of plenty—before that all you can see is rice,' she counseled:

But there is no hopeless entanglement for those who put in the effort, only for those who do not understand and wait for a miracle, those who never grow up and live 'by chance' and without direction… I know that the resignation you voice is part of what you're experiencing right now. But by accepting our present reality without self-pity, we already overcome that resentment and open doors to the world outside. I believe one must have patience and confidence. Something always *comes along*, Georg, on levels we don't perceive and like physical growth in gradual stages we don't notice. All at once, we've grown out of our circumstances just as children outgrow their clothes. Only if we refuse to grow and employ our lives, only if we let ourselves be pushed down the path of least resistance—in that case we will encounter no twist of fate, and no doors will open up.

I write about this at such length because I find all this very fulfilling, as metaphysical idea and experienced reality. It's not long ago that I was sitting on my bed at the Philippis' home on Mendelssohnstrasse 49 in Frankfurt feeling hopelessly enslaved. No fairy-tale prince is coming to save us, but life, experience, our readiness and confidence—there is an indescribably beautiful passage in the Bible: 'Faith is the assurance of what we do not hope for [sic!] and the certainty of what we do not see.' Hoping is *arbitrary anticipation*, as though one tried to know the fruit before the tree even had leaves. Meanwhile, confidence is simultaneously knowing of the past and future just as we living beings know of death.—I love life very much, Georg. Not for the sake of happiness, but for the wonderful possibilities it offers to develop and transform oneself. For what is unhappiness but a withdrawal from the task of change. In this sense, it's impossible to be unhappy. Everything can be changed. The process can be carried out with every material. There is nothing that cannot be overcome. 'Only the flame burns, not the fuel.'[55]

The philosophy of personalism and Guardini's reformed Catholic teachings about individual freedom and the authority of conscience contributed to Helene's growing estrangement from Germany in the months after she penned these words: Nazism was on the rise, and this initially caused a conflict with her brother. However, Guardini's idea of 'community' was ill-suited to defending Weimar democracy. On the contrary, it ignored the fact that perceived commonalities were infused not only with cultural and historical differences, but also with concrete conflicts of interest that needed to be dealt with politically, with democratic procedures and the rule of law.[56]

The period from winter 1930 through the first half of 1931 gave Helene ample opportunity to test the resilience of her ideas. As Kurt Wolff wrote to his friend Hans Mardersteig, he was forced to wait 'in this time of the deepest depression of the economy and the state' instead of seeking a new job, which would only have brought 'inevitable rejections'. The dissolution of the Kurt Wolff Publishing House, the bones of which were left in the hands of his ex-wife's brother-in-law, Peter Reinhold, was delayed by the economic crisis. He still owed money to Pantheon. And while he also had to manage a 'deluge of correspondence', he suffered from having 'nothing "proper", nourishing and productive to do'. He complained to Mardersteig: 'I cannot tell you how I long for a reasonable occupation that approximates my—non-exaggerated—capabilities and talents. I can assure you that if I used to be demanding on the subject in regard to "elevated position and salary", those days are over. The only thing important to me is a chance to work.'[57] Helene benefited from Wolff's new-found modesty, a result of his willingness to change. No longer did he just buy curtains for her. He also did the dishes and made the bed. His divorce had also been finalized. Nonetheless, the 'many unbridgeable differences' that still existed between the two of them took her to the verge of a nervous breakdown.[58] While Wolff traveled with his ex-wife and their children to Engadin and planned a restorative vacation in Menton for the spring to recover from the after-effects of fish poisoning, Helene in Paris went hungry to save money to send to her mother and sister in Munich.

As of 1931, Helene no longer worked for Reece. Instead, she had a job as a secretary for a branch of the League of Nations, the Institut International de Coopération Intellectuelle. Yet although she had escaped the unhealthy atmosphere of Pantheon, and working outside Wolff's sphere of influence had improved her self-esteem, her job 'typing idiotic resolutions' bored her, taxed her physically and offered no prospects of a life together with the man she loved.[59] Wolff 'beseeched' her to quit her job for her health, but that carried the risk of her becoming dependent on him again.[60] Helene decided to take this risk in the spring of 1931, accompanying Wolff to southern France. But she hedged her bets in two senses, by getting her employer to grant her two months' unpaid leave and by keeping her apartment on Boulevard Saint-Michel. If the 'experiment' of living together with Wolff 'proved happy', then she would 'stay with him—otherwise, back to Paris'. Her talents as a secretary, in great demand on the market, strengthened her hand after the two months were over, and she made her final decision to stay by Wolff's side. The fact that she had work she didn't want and he wanted work he didn't have also helped mitigate the asymmetry and inequality of their relationship.

Helene's 'experiment' during her two-month sabbatical was about not just living together with Wolff but also embarking on a project of her own that should eventually create another income for herself: to test whether she could realize the dream inherited from her mother of making a career of writing. Two months, she felt, would be enough to complete a play. Wolff was the only one she took into her confidence from the start about this endeavor, and he supported her in every respect. Helene derived the confidence needed for her project both from her conviction that she was a good writer and from literary trends at the time which enabled a young generation of women writers in the late 1920s to draw on their experience of changing gender roles and office culture and bring it to the stage. In the early 1930s, Helene had no problem with her literary efforts not living up to the ideal of 'world literature'. She wrote to her brother: 'I understand that according to absolute standards, measured against Sophocles and Shakespeare, I'm a meaningless bag of wind. But in the end, Georg, I'm reflecting the world, even if it's only my own world. And reality, too, has its rights—a reality that's intentionally undramatic and that intentionally elides over and over into everyday life.'[61]

When Helene joined Kurt Wolff in Menton during the first days of April 1931, she was confronted by a new situation, one which he had brought about in the previous two weeks and which was as threatening to her first experiment (living together) as it was inspiring for her second (writing). Wolff had a new lover. Manon Neven Dumont was a radiant, elegant woman ten years Helene's senior who was then living in her mother's vacation home in Gairaut in the hills above Nice. This triangular constellation and its consequences would be part of the story in *Background for Love*. Wolff suggested to both women that they jointly rent a house and try living together, leaving Helene with no option but to accept another ménage à trois. While Wolff and Dumont scoured the coast between Menton and Marseilles in search of a suitable property for the summer, Helene was paid a visit from Georg, who met her lover in person for the first time and returned to Germany quite critical of the dissolute lifestyle of German cosmopolitans on the coast of southern France. Helene initially used her real-life love triangle for a play. It was called *Trio* and featured only three characters: HE (forty-four years old), SHE (thirty-four) and IT (twenty-four), a *garçonne*, more androgynous than asexual, an observing, reflective and conciliatory creature, while HE and SHE were victims of masculine and feminine impulsivity. In the play, the three pick on each other at a weekend retreat, although in a light, joking tone. The action is restricted entirely to their relationship. But *Trio* was more than just light entertainment. It staked a claim to 'intellectual topicality' and aspired to reflect and confront the audience with a piece of 'reality'. Wolff described the reaction of the writer Karl Wolfskehl to the manuscript, which he had sent without revealing the author, as follows: 'It struck him as a play of extreme topicality in terms of situation and mentality, forty years after Strindberg. In its scenic conception, it wasn't a light conversation piece but rather, in the hands of the right director, a work filled with a dreadful and disillusioned view of the present day.'[62]

By 1st May, Wolff had found the property he was looking for: Villa Voisin on the outskirts of Saint-Tropez, a fishing village on the peninsula between Toulon and Cannes. 'Everything theatrical and stagey about the Côte d'Azur proper is absent,' he wrote to Mardersteig. 'You feel surrounded by nature amidst wine, corn, figs, olives, cork trees and forests that stretch all the way down to most marvelously pure sandy beach. There are no hotels, no shops of any kind, just a couple of 2- to 5-room houses that can be rented as a whole or room by room, and nothing else.'[63] On 15th May he, Dumont and Helene moved into Villa Voisin together. But the constellation was intolerable in such close confines. After only a few days, Helene found accommodation of her own in a small cottage, or *cabanon*, nearby. It had a well out front and was located on a vineyard, exactly as she would later describe in *Background for Love*. Here she was able to finish her play by the end of the month.

In early July she sought to explain to her brother what things were like between her, Wolff and Dumont and what future prospects kept her from exercising the option to return to Paris:

You can come any time you want, Georg. You will not feel any tension between Kurt and me or Manon and me, nor any conflict. I will tell you sometime in detail how everything happened, but it is truly 'grown over'. And it's strange how we will carry on. You know that I stepped back. I wanted to leave and go back to Paris or somewhere where I could devote myself to new work and leave Kurt and Manon to themselves. But they didn't want that, *either* of them, so I only removed myself 500 meters, to my little house amidst the grapevines. I have *let go completely* of Kurt. In the weeks and months we have been here I have only seen him and her together, never, or almost never, him alone. We have taken a couple of walks together — that's it. He lives entirely with the other woman. Manon is infinitely nice, but she is very much a woman. She suffered a lot from our initial attempt to live as a threesome. I can admit this to you. You might understand. I love Kurt so much that I could leave entirely. We have a level of internal connection that can easily do without external confirmation for a time... My dear brother, the strange thing is that the more I let go of Kurt externally, the stronger he feels connected to me. That may sound paradoxical, but no one suffers from separation more than Kurt. With Manon and him, it doesn't work. They have no everyday life together… You are allowed to be sad, but you can't claim any 'rights'. Perhaps you now understand my disinclination toward marriage. It's a form of possessiveness in matters that must remain entirely voluntary and up in the air. It's not that I have no appreciation for faithfulness, but when I ask for faithfulness by citing 'rights', that is wrong. I must experience it, earn it through love and not hope for it. I had a rare conversation with Kurt yesterday, and I felt afterward that his 'unfaithfulness' brought me closer to faithfulness. He will perhaps live together with Manon for some more weeks, maybe even months. But he will never be 'together' with her, and this relationship will someday change because of mutual exhaustion. Manon is a woman whom one marries, and Kurt a man whom one doesn't marry. In the long term, Manon will not be able to endure that.[64]

That was precisely what happened. On 6th July, Wolff returned to Germany to take care of personal matters in Berlin and Munich and pick up his children and their nanny for the summer holidays. Before he left, he assured Helene that everything between Dumont and him was 'irrevocably over'.[65] She remained for a time in Villa Voisin, and Helene kept the *cabanon*, but as of the end of July no mention was made of her in either Wolff's calendar or Helene's letters. Her name wouldn't crop up again until the spring of 1932—when Helene referred to her as a close friend who lived with her children in Garmisch and was wealthy and generous enough to offer Helene's struggling relatives all sorts of help. In any case, she took a decisive step forward with Wolff in the summer of 1931:

> I sense ever more strongly the uncompromising destiny of this connection whose actual significance will only become clear over the course of years... Marriage is communion with or without a trip to city hall. I'm prepared to make our communion a reality. Sometimes it looks as though Kurt were capable of this as well, but I have stopped believing words. Perhaps we will live together. Perhaps someday for simplicity's sake we will get married. But we already *belong together*. Kurt still lacks the strength to make this a reality. But he no longer lacks the awareness.[66]

During the ten days in Munich and Berlin, in which Wolff worked on the dissolution of his publishing house, managed his money, went to a notary and met with his ex-wife, friends and acquaintances, he found crisis-battered Germany at a new low point. On 13th July 1931, several banks declared insolvency after businesses went belly-up, Germans transferred money outside the country and foreign credit was called in. Fearing that they were about to lose their savings for the second time in a generation, people stormed financial institutions. The Brüning government tried to get the crisis under control by issuing presidential decrees. Among the measures ordered were obstacles to transferring assets abroad. An international conference was convened in London to save the German economy by negotiating foreign credit extensions. Walter Hasenclever, who was in Berlin at the time, urged Wolff to leave Germany as soon as he could: 'I beseech you. Don't waste a minute with your departure. The situation in Germany, should London fail, can become a catastrophe overnight. *Don't delay*.'[67]

There is no surviving documentation about how exactly Wolff financed his stays in France and how he got his money across the borders. We know that in the early 1930s he had money deposited at an English and a Swiss bank. With Pantheon Casa Editrice, he had held foreign investments since 1924. We do not know whether he transferred assets out of Germany for which he would have been liable to pay penalties under the retroactively instituted Reich Flight Tax. In October 1931 he was no longer able to send the money he had in Germany to France or exchange it for francs. Hasenclever had also spread his assets between several European countries. From that point on the two men helped one another, using complicated transactions. Once, Wolff had his secretary in Munich send 1,000 marks to Hasenclever in Berlin, who was supposed to pay him the equivalent in francs. 'Someone somewhere in the world must owe you money,' Wolff wrote to Hasenclever.[68] A month later, in November 1931, a priority letter from his ex-wife Elisabeth summoned him immediately to Munich, where he again went to a notary and, according to his calendar, met every day with a fellow named Wesley Long, whom he had also seen frequently the previous July. Because ownership of the remainder of the Kurt Wolff Publishing House was transferred to Elisabeth's brother-in-law, Peter Reinhold, in the latter half of 1931 but his name doesn't appear at all in Wolff's 1931 calendar, it can be assumed that Long was involved in these transactions. In December, back in southern France, Wolff visited Barclays Bank in Nice almost daily. A short time later, in February 1932, he and Helene traveled via Paris to London, where they stayed for ten days in an unheated hotel room. There they met several times with Ron Rubenstein, a London lawyer with good connections to English banks. Helcne called the trip a 'strenuous pilgrimage with a dubious result'.[69] Wolff then traveled alone to Munich, again meeting with Long and returning to southern France after a detour through Berlin and Bonn. In the meantime, his secretary in Munich had 'so overworked herself that she had a nervous breakdown'.[70] It's likely that Wolff succeeded in transferring the money earned from the sale of his publishing house to England via a middleman. In July 1932 he noted in his calendar, after Rubinstein had called: '6,000 pounds approved.'

Wolff spent all fall and winter of 1931–32 fretting about the remnants of his wealth, which at least partly explains his restlessness. Helene meanwhile took responsibility for organizing the households they had on the Côte d'Azur, so they kept costs down yet could remain charming and generous hosts to their increasing number of guests. With the departure of Dumont, and with their stay in France seeming less like a vacation and more like exile, Helene's position at Wolff's side was reinforced. We don't know whether she was introduced to his children as their future stepmother when they came to visit. In any case, by September 1931 Wolff's guests considered her his domestic partner. Two people were particularly close to Wolff and Helene: Hasenclever, who brought along a rotating cast of girlfriends, and a young, single woman named Mila, who kept a small monkey as a pet and earned her keep with commissions for advertising designs. 'Mila pours cherry liqueur over pink peaches, petite Helene serves artfully decorated bowls with her delicate hands, and the cat mews,' was how Hasenclever described the idyllic evenings shared by their vacation community.[71] But the group were also united by their horror at the situation unfolding in Germany and their feelings of homelessness, which made their circle seem increasingly like an emergency arrangement, even if the sun, the sea and the fine food prepared every night by Joséphine, an illiterate farmgirl from Antibes, would have made it seem tasteless and gauche to show depression or 'mortal fear' within the group.[72] At the end of September 1931 Hasenclever returned to Berlin, ostensibly because he missed the lovely ladies of the city. Meanwhile, Wolff felt 'quite abandoned… when you don't get world events interpreted for you in a circle of chatting men'.[73]

In 1930–31, Kurt Wolff, Helene and their guests were the only Germans in Saint-Tropez. Two of their neighbors were the famous French author Colette and the painter André Dunoyer de Segonzac.[74] Other German artists and intellectuals had for similar reasons also discovered the French Riviera, settling in different places. The author Julius Meier-Graefe and the painter Annemarie Meier-Graefe, his wife, came in 1930 to Sanary-sur-Mer, where Aldous Huxley and other English notables had formed an intellectual colony. Meanwhile, the Austrian writer Emil Alphons Rheinhardt had lived since 1928 in Le

Lavandou, a bit east of Toulon.[75] Wolff knew the Meier-Graefes, Huxley and the others from the halcyon days of his publishing house, but he had little social contact with them. The Wolffs did have several friends in Nice whom they saw frequently: an impoverished painter named Rolfe Memison, who went around with a ukulele and who was immortalized in *Background for Love*; a certain 'Rechberg', probably the industrialist, sculptor and conservative democrat Arnold Rechberg, who had lived for years in Paris and was known as a private advocate of German-French and German-British reconciliation and a staunch critic of the Soviet Union; and a Frenchwoman named Madeleine de Burbure, who supported Helene when she had to have her appendix removed in Nice in the fall of 1931.

Wolff had more valuable business connections in Italy and Switzerland. They included his old friend the art book printer Hans Mardersteig in Verona and the art historian and collector Bernard Berenson, together with his women and entourage in Fiesole near Florence. Baron Curt von Faber du Faur, and for a time Karl Wolfskehl, also lived in the area, while Baron Kurd von Hardt, who advised Wolff financially, maintained a splendid estate not far from Geneva. Wolff and Helene embarked on a six-week trip through Italy in November and December 1931. In addition to visiting '170 churches with their obligatory art', the journey was an opportunity to find out whether there was any work for Wolff in Italy and to gather opinions on Helene's play *Trio*.[76] While Wolff spent a few days in Munich dealing with his finances, Helene stayed with Hans Mardersteig and his wife in Verona and enthusiastically did some editing for his press. Both Wolff and Helene were constantly on the lookout for editing and translation work. But the situation in Italy turned out to be so unfavorable that, as Helene wrote to Mardersteig, they lacked the 'courage' to settle down anywhere and had to 'stand, for the time being, constantly at the ready in destiny's hotel'.[77]

It didn't matter in any meaningful way that Italy had a fascist government, although they were aware of the unpleasant dominance of the state. Wolff wrote to Hasenclever: 'Italy is a fundamentally very beautiful country, but compared to France, it is horribly state-centered. When I think about how we lived in Saint-Tropez for six months without registering with the authorities, whereas here you can never let go of your *passaporto*, the macaroni and ravioli, which, after all, you can also get in neighboring countries, pale in significance.'[78] The apolitical attitudes of Kurt Wolff and Helene at the time toward fascism are hard to understand today. Shortly before they set off on their Italian trip from Saint-Tropez, Wolff had enjoyed reading Franz Werfel's latest novel *Die Geschwister von Neapel* (*The Siblings of Naples*), which was set in Italy. He praised it to Mardersteig as 'a marvelous book, playful and transcendent… towering over the rest of Werfel's prose'.[79] It depicted Italian fascism as a brutal, inhumane, capricious, corrupt yet somehow metaphysically necessary part of modernism. In any case, we can say that Wolff and Helene, without sympathizing with fascism in any way, accepted living in fascist Italy far more easily than in chaotic, desperate, yet semi-democratic Germany. Still under influence of his trip to Berlin and Munich, Wolff wrote from

Italy to Hasenclever, who was in Sweden at the time, working on the play *Christopher Columbus: or the Discovery of America* with his friend Kurt Tucholsky: 'My dear fellow, the atmosphere in Germany surely is hopeless and revolting. You feel it after five minutes. I can't imagine you wanting to stay in Berlin for any length of time, with its apocalyptic-mood-turned-mass-psychosis, after you finish your work in Sweden. (I don't know why but while in Munich I had to think of August 1914, the mood was the same, although the situation was reversed.) The women may be sweet, but you can't live from that alone. I mean the short nights don't seem to me to be reason enough to tolerate long, shitty days.' Helene, who had not returned to Germany but had followed events there in the newspapers, added in the same letter: 'Tucho [Tucholsky] must be beside himself after the Ossietzky trial.[80] We are as well. Hopefully such measures will not force you to pull a lot of punches in *Columbus*. With this sort of judicial interpretation, there's a lot that can be gone after as treason, especially when a *Weltbühne* editor has infected the work with his poisonous and base spirit. What a country! The livable world is getting smaller and smaller.'[81] In fact, Hasenclever had no intention of returning to Berlin, and Italy was no option for him either. 'No, my dear children, we belong in southern France,' he replied. 'I share Kurt's nausea with Germany.' He ended his letter with a prediction that exceeded all of Wolff and Helene's worst fears: 'Tucho and I have a grim view of our fatherland. The game is up. We face exile, bans and public contempt—off to France. The homeless have to stick together!!'[82]

Wolff and Helene were still ambivalent about Germany, though. Both became defensive whenever accused of having abandoned the country in its hour of need and selfishly distancing themselves from Germans' collective fate. Wolff characterized the situation to Mardersteig:

Whenever I read about and feel the ever darker, more threatening and more ominous German situation in letters, newspapers and conversations, I am increasingly occupied by the question of whether my current form of life is permissible, or whether it amounts to running away from a collective destiny. But no matter how seriously and intensely I ponder the situation, I can see no sense in heading to Berlin or any other German city. All my thoughts in this direction remain a vicious circle, a cat that bites its own tail. It is indeed a horrible Europe in which we live.[83]

For Helene, Georg was primarily the one to whom she had to defend herself. 'I want you to see our life correctly,' she wrote. 'It is not a life of luxury between blue skies and sun. It's a simple life between two people who love one another, who are "happy" because they don't torment each other and who have, temporarily at least, all of life's necessities. You've almost certainly gotten the wrong idea. This is not a terribly egotistical existence.'[84]

Helene didn't know and didn't ask, but she could well have suspected that her brother, who was still doing his apprenticeship at IG Farben in Frankfurt, had assumed responsibility not just for their mother, who also regularly received money from Wolff and Helene, and their sister Ena, whom Helene dismissed as a 'bottomless hole' and refused to continue supporting, but also for their estranged father in Berlin, who had intensified his efforts to extract money with blackmail.[85] Helene refused to hear his name spoken in her presence. On the other hand, Wolff and Helene had succeeded in 1931 in improving her mother and Ena's living situation. They had moved from their miserable attic apartment to a larger one on Munich's English Garden whose main tenant was Annemarie von Puttkamer. Helene's mother ran the household for her and her other subletters. In return, she and Ena had the run of two bedrooms and a living room. But Helene was still burdened by the questions of what the future would hold for the family in Germany, how Ena could be provided for, how Georg would cope with a hated job forced upon him by material necessity, and what would become of their youngest sister Liesel. These unresolved issues bound Helene to Germany, just as Wolff's two children did him as well.

Money was the main reason why Wolff and Helene quit Italy in December 1931 and again began looking for somewhere to live in southern France. The Depression had caused a massive drop in prices and rents. 'Everything has gotten insanely cheap here,' Helene wrote to Georg. 'You can rent as many houses as you want.'[86] Conditions were ideal for finding 'something Voisin-like', where they could 'ripen with cheerful friends à la Mila-Walter toward our final bankruptcy'.[87] For the winter, she and Wolff moved into a house in Cagnes-sur-Mer near Nice, 'built into the old city wall with early Renaissance walls and lovely, authentic beam ceilings, twisting staircases, deep windows and a marvelous view over the hills of olive trees' to the Maritime Alps. It also had central heating, running water and guest rooms.[88] Without any great difficulty, they procured *cartes d'identité.* Their first guests were Memison and the Bavarian writer Claire Goll, the wife of the poet Yvan Goll and an ex-lover of Rainer Maria Rilke. She was also an ex-lover of Wolff from his Leipzig days, and Helene would later recall her as 'melodramatic and intentionally overwrought to the point of being shrill and tasteless'.[89] In contrast to Memison, Claire Goll was a paying guest and had to be pampered and taken care of as a psychosomatic who had threatened suicide ever since her husband had confessed to an affair with a fellow poet. During her stay in the house she completed a novel with the telling title *Arsenic*, a story of jealousy which Wolff helped her finish. 'The last chapter is almost entirely by him,' Goll wrote to her husband. 'I couldn't continue. Everything always becomes so clear when you speak with him, the new novel as well. You know immediately what you must do.'[90]

After their trip to London, with Wolff occupied in Munich and Berlin, Helene traveled without him to Cagnes. She was accompanied by Hasenclever, who was 'short on money' and 'happy that dear Helene—guardian angel to us all—operates the household on the cheap'.[91] Another house guest was Wolff's Munich secretary, who was trying to recover from her nervous breakdown. 'Just being outside Germany is medicine,' Helene wrote to Mardersteig.[92] At the same time, perhaps buoyed by his successful editing of Claire Goll's novel, Wolff was abundantly aware that he couldn't spend another year doing nothing but arranging his finances and lazing around. When in Cagnes he spent his days shopping, going for walks, writing letters and looking at vacation homes. Sometimes he played chess with Hasenclever, after which he would read a book and in the evening go out, alone or with others, in Nice to dine on *boeuf à la mode* or to socialize. On 24th February 1932, Helene wrote to Mardersteig:

> Kurt can't spend another winter divorced from the world as he's doing now. You're right. He needs to either find or invent for himself some work. But he'll never do that here. Left to his own devices, he's entirely unproductive. It often seems to me that this is his fundamental nature, and the only way he gets things done is as a mediator—in this sense his work thus far has been symbolic. As long as he lives 'out in the desert', he's out of his life's element. He can neither transmit nor receive. For that reason, we are determined to depart the coast at the latest by this fall and move back north, either to Berlin or Paris. I'm a bit afraid of that but fear of course does no good.[93]

Unlike Wolff, Helene benefited from 'life in the desert' with its calm, space and lots of time. She had something to occupy herself with, namely her writing, and could see a future in it. Wolff took up her cause and freely used his contacts on her behalf. At a time when Hasenclever, still in Germany, believed rumors that his friend had married Manon Dumont, Wolff sent him the manuscript of Helene's play, asking him to read it carefully and give feedback: 'This is an appeal from a friend. An unexpected but urgent one.'[94] Hasenclever, however, was not to ask about the identity of the author. He first believed that Wolff was himself the playwright and congratulated him effusively, calling the play 'an excellent dialogue about a highly interesting, tremendously modern relationship between vivid characters that has never before been depicted on stage this sharply and unambiguously'.[95] As a potential agent, he recommended his sister Marita in Berlin, 'who works for that sort of office and works closely with [publishers] Ullstein, Deutsche Verlagsanstalt, Kiepenheuer, etc.'.[96] Marita did indeed later become Helene's agent, and Walter Hasenclever became Helene's literary teacher and advisor after arriving in Saint-Tropez and discovering the truth. While Wolff was trying out living with Dumont, Helene and Walter spent afternoons in the *cabanon* revising her play. By that time, Annemarie von Puttkamer also had a copy of the manuscript. Hasenclever always encouraged and supported her in her desire not only to write but to earn a living from it. Helene thus felt very much at ease. As she wrote her brother, she hoped to 'earn Mama's supplement with this activity, since the financial problems need be solved soon and the prospect of being able to do this with freelance work as a writer is quite nice'. If Wolff was still together with Dumont when his children arrived, she told Georg, perhaps she would travel to Menton with Hasenclever. 'H. has truly become attached to me and needs someone to make sure he doesn't eat too much.'[97] At the same time, she knew as well that the times were hardly auspicious for literary projects.[98]

The biggest difficulty in finding a publisher or distributor for the play was Helene's insistence on using the pseudonym 'Stefan Palm', a playwright ostensibly living in isolation and too shy to appear in public. Helene wrote of her avatar to Marita Hasenclever: 'He is 25 years old and hails not from Vienna but southern Germany. Beside the comedy, which will certainly be finished by January, the author is also working on an ambitious novel, which is unlikely to be completed prior to the end of 1931.'[99] Marita passed on this information to German publishers. In November 1931 the play was under consideration at Chronos, the theatrical imprint of Deutsche Verlagsanstalt in Stuttgart. Helene's ex-fiancé Alf, who was then working as a set designer, composer and film music advisor, tried to get his friends in the world of stage interested in the comedy. During various trips through France and Italy, Wolff and Helene read from the play to friends trusted to know that she was the author. They placed particular store by the opinion of Faber du Faur in Florence. The fact that he was 'very passionately impressed' encouraged Wolff to pressure Marita into hurrying up and devoting more energy to the project.[100] For his part, Faber du Faur enlisted Karl Wolfskehl, who had also withdrawn to Florence in the face of the 'completely poisoned atmosphere of the soul' in Germany.[101] Wolff and Helene had met with him when they visited the Italian city, and Wolfskehl was so taken with her and the positive transformation she had wrought upon Kurt that he promised, without having read the play, to put in a good word for it with German theaters. 'Allow me to say, and please repeat it further, that to me Kurt Wolff has never been as close, familiar and more completely a friend as this time around,' Wolfskehl wrote to Helene:

> It would be lovely if our plan bore fruit and your play could in fact be sold. I hold Curt von Faber's critical eye in very high regard, he told me repeatedly in very exact, enthusiastic and objective terms about your work. He considers it eminently ready for the stage, so I'm happy—and not just for reasons of friendship—to perhaps do something for it. Of course, I'll have to look at it first but perhaps it's not too late for this season. There's no predicting the future, naturally. What isn't up in the air and unclear in these troubled times? But we have to accept that and remain true to ourselves and above all our strengths![102]

By mid-February 1932, Marita Hasenclever and Chronos had agreed a contract concerning the play, and a few weeks later she was able to arrange for 'Stefan Palm', as was mandatory at the time, to join the Association of German Theatrical Authors and Composers. The first theater that showed a 'lively' interest in the play was the Dresden Staatstheater, but it ultimately decided against *Trio* because it was felt that a three-person comedy was too small for such a large house.[103]

Why did Helene insist on a pseudonym? Faber du Faur, Wolfskehl and several other friends knew about her writing, but one of Wolff's closest friends, Mardersteig, did not, even though he had been one of the first people introduced to her as the new main woman at Wolff's side and Wolff had thanked him for the 'kindness with which you became the first to receive this person—nearest and dearest to me though completely unknown to you'.[104] One reason for the secrecy, along with the frivolity of the play, might have been Reece. Since Wolff had left Pantheon, their personal relationship had returned to normal. He and Helene saw Reece and his wife Jeanne regularly in Paris, Florence and Nice. Reece was as active as ever as the publisher of Pegasus Press in the French capital, and a short time previously he had started a new endeavor with the German publisher Christian Wegner, the Albatross Continental Library, which marketed English-language books outside the US and Britain.[105] Because of Wolff's poor English and the freshness of the two men's only recently overcome conflict vis-à-vis Pantheon, Wolff took no part in this project. Helene's situation was different. She had already done translation from English, and Reece regarded her highly as an editor, secretary and translator. Should she want to work again for him, it may have seemed better if he didn't know about her literary ambitions for the time being.

Having determined that their life in the southern European sun would come to end one way or another come fall, Wolff and Helene planned two trips for the interval. They wanted to see the rest of Provence outside Marseilles, Spain, then the Balearic Islands and parts of North Africa. On 25th April 1932 they quit Cagnes, storing the majority of their thirty trunks of personal possessions in the *cabanon*, and went to Le Lavandou, where Hasenclever had rented a house. There they were introduced to Marita and met Tucholsky. Together with Marita and Rolfe

Memison they traveled to Barcelona and caught the ferry to Majorca, where they spent a week sunbathing on the beach, taking excursions and shopping for ceramics, one of Wolff's particular passions. Upon returning to France they settled into the *cabanon*, where Helene had lived alone for the past year and where they would now spend the summer together.

Meanwhile, Hasenclever's house in Le Lavandou had become a magnet for further German expats: along with Marita and Tucholsky, the writer Rudolf Leonhard and Reinhold and Gerda Schairer, he a pedagogue and a co-founder and director of the German Students' Association and she a woman who also harbored literary ambitions. Hasenclever and Tucholsky had completed their Columbus play, and Hasenclever was now working on another stage piece, *Happiness of the Senses and Peace of the Soul*, about the suffering of a Marseilles prostitute murdered by her pimp.[106] Wolff and Helene sometimes took day trips to Le Lavandou, and on one occasion the entire clique visited them in their *cabanon*. Tucholsky was even more pessimistic about the situation in Germany than Hasenclever. Gerda Schairer recalled: '[He suffered] a lot because he couldn't breathe through his nose properly. He was very quiet, almost melancholy. Now and again, when he read something in the newspaper that enraged him and demanded to be let out, his anger would explode.'[107]

The German population in Sanary-sur-Mer was also increasing. René Schickele arrived for a month with his family in the spring of 1932 to have a look around the 'heavenly coast'. It wasn't until late August that he contacted Wolff, asking his help in locating accommodation. Wolff suggested Cagnes and helpfully alerted him to the 'wealth of enchanting and inexpensive properties' in Saint-Tropez. But the Schickeles opted for Sanary because their good friends the Meier-Graefes lived there.[108] Wolff and Helene rarely went to Sanary, although they enjoyed cordial relations with the Schickeles. Mostly, they preferred to remain around Nice with their own guests.

It is impossible to overlook the fact that Wolff was rather isolated from most of his former authors and the literary and art scene that flocked to the French Riviera in 1932 and 1933. In June 1932, having asked Mardersteig for his address, Hermann Hesse mailed him a card because he felt that 'it must be a rough time for you' and wanted to send 'some small amusement or greeting'. Wolff responded effusively: 'My dearly esteemed Hermann Hesse, it's like a bit of magic. Here I am living in a remote corner of southern France, completely still and private, and suddenly I am called by name, and words make their way to me that are intended entirely for me personally. Yes, it is a form of magic, but in my current form of life, which will lead I know not where, I have learnt that magic is real. I have also understood that gifts received are completely undeserved, but one can offer thanks for them anyway. Is that not so?'[109] It was this ability to 'learn' and 'understand' that made Helene defend Wolff, despite all his vices and flaws, as a man capable of and willing to change.

For the time being, his life as a changed and changing man remained restricted to his private circle. As of mid-July, he and Helene were deluged by visiting family members from

Germany. To accommodate at least some of them, the couple rented Villa Schlumberger in Saint-Tropez, a beachside house with plenty of space but without electricity or running water. For six weeks it was home to Wolff's children, fourteen-year-old Maria and eleven-year-old Niko, together with their nanny. Now they realized that Helene was their future stepmother, and they did their best to provoke her by being 'quite difficult'.[110] The sister of Wolff's ex-wife and various other divorced or non-divorced relatives also visited, as did Helene's mother, nicknamed 'Zita' or 'Zitchen', whom Wolff had specially invited so that she could recover from the privations of her life in Munich. For Helene, it was 'crucially important' that Wolff and her mother got along and that the latter be integrated into her new social circles. Zita's visit was a test, not for Zita but for Wolff, who had already sent 300 marks that year to Munich. 'He passed "the exam" with flying colors and has been promoted to the next grade of human being with top marks,' wrote Helene. 'Kurt loves Zitchen and told me the evening after she left that she could live with us as long as she wanted, not just 4 weeks, as long we have some place to live ourselves.'[111] The more solidified Helene's relationship with Wolff became, the harder she worked on getting her family out of Germany and at her side. She racked her brains as to how to enable Liesel to visit, and she hoped Georg would come again and correct the bad impression he had taken from Menton. 'You could use a bit of airing out,' she wrote to him. 'Munich isn't the right place. Always the same filth. It's lovely here. You'd like Kurt a lot more. He is continually getting simpler, milder and more natural. And I want you to have an accurate view of our lives.'[112]

Her insistence on bringing her close relatives to France was entirely in keeping with her attempts since childhood to educate her family and lift them up socially, but the project had also taken on a political dimension. In the depths of his emotional depression, Georg in Frankfurt had concluded that individuals had no choice but to submit to the collective and meekly join its ranks. Seduced by Nietzsche and above all Stefan George, in his letters he began advocating nationalism and the rights of nations to defend themselves. Helene tried to convince him otherwise:

At bottom, all of this is compensation, or a flight from the void of a soulless world to something that at least has form and shape. I'm of a different opinion than you. I don't believe that for people like you and me subordination to military discipline is the only salvation from chaos. I also think that nationalism will be overcome just as the separation of people into cities and tribes has been. You say that if we don't strike first, the other side will. In Germany, France is always what's meant by 'the other side'—the same nation that despite the massive wave of nationalism in Germany voted for Herriot and not Tardieu. It's curious. I live here in a land whose inhabitants mostly support moderation, as the elections showed. You live there in a land that is passionately throwing itself into the arms of patriotic rabble-rousers. It makes no sense to write of these things. I can only hope that you, whose secret longing for substance and some form to his life I understand, will not simply grab the first best option. It's so endlessly important that the few selfless and well-intentioned people don't lose their way and bring the 'strength of their idealism' into the wrong camp.

I am writing to you from this lovely, still, wonderfully fertile landscape that has so become home to me that I feel no longing whatever for any other country. You will see that as betrayal. I know that you too would be different—more moderate, life-affirming, cheerful and open—if you could enjoy the gift of such a free life in such expansive nature. But this is not under our control. I only urge you: try not to become fanatical, ossified and stiff despite the many shortcomings of your external life.[113]

Eight days after Helene wrote these words, President Paul von Hindenburg dissolved the German parliament, the Reichstag. From that point on Germany was governed by Franz von Papen, whom Hindenburg had installed as Reich chancellor together with a cabinet of 'national concentration'. They were only able to rule by emergency decree. On 14th July 1932, Papen's regime rescinded acknowledgement of the Social Democratic government of Prussia, which had governed provisionally after an inconclusive regional election, and named Papen Reich commissar of that most powerful German regional state. In the run-up to a fresh Reichstag election, the atmosphere had become more and more like that of a civil war, particularly after Papen rescinded the ban on the SA and SS so that the

Nazis would tolerate his regime. On 20th July, Hindenburg and Papen's de facto coup d'état in Prussia was complete. A state of emergency was declared, and the previous government driven out of office. It was on this day that Wolff, for the first time, noted anything political in his calendar: '10:30 radio: state of siege in Berlin.' The national elections of 31st July 1932 brought no majority for either the conservative, monarchist restoration policies of Hindenburg, Papen and their ilk or for the democratic parties that supported the Weimar Republic. The Nazi Party garnered 37.3 per cent of the vote, becoming the biggest parliamentary group in the Reichstag. Fear of a German civil war, and especially of a communist revolution, made a regime including the Nazis seem like the lesser of two evils to many people who had not voted for the party and considered Hitler an uneducated prole.

The Reichstag election destroyed one of Wolff's plans of going back to work in Germany, which had temporarily given him some future perspective. Lilly Ackermann, an acting coach and friend of Marita Hasenclever, who resided in Berlin, wanted to establish a theater to premiere new plays, and Wolff had been envisioned as its head. A conceptual outline had been drawn up, Ackermann and Marita had done some 'preparatory publicity work', letters had been exchanged, and the hope was that it would be easier to finance the theater with the end of the German reparation payments negotiated at the 1932 Lausanne Conference. But the election meant that those plans were dropped.[114] Another idea was even shorter-lived. That September, Wolff believed for a couple of days that Reinhold

Schairer could use his connections in Berlin to secure him a position at the head of a radio station. At that moment, the German Interior Ministry was beginning to nationalize and centralize private radio broadcasters and appoint a state commissar to supervise them. The chief motivation for the Papen regime to do this was to bypass the German parliament and German newspapers and communicate directly with the rapidly growing numbers of radio listeners in the country. The new radio organization was a major step on the road to state-dominated Nazi radio.[115] It is no longer clear what 'illustrious post' might have been open to Wolff and why Hasenclever considered him 'absolutely predisposed' to fill it.[116] In any case, it quickly emerged that Schairer's connections weren't as good as hoped, and Wolff decided it no longer made sense to travel to Berlin at short notice.

Helene also became increasingly political in the wake of the election and drew conclusions about the growing influence of the Nazis for her own future as an author in Germany. A new play she wrote in the summer of 1932—entitled *Haus Nervenruh* (*House Calmness of Nerves*)—was so full of polyamorous flirtation and so saucy that she could never expect to have any success with it in Germany. At most it could be read aloud in Marita's home in Berlin, 'assuming that there is no emergency order banning even such events by then'.[117] Helene asked Mirita, ironically, whether any 'Heil Hitler plays' had arrived at her agency, and Marita countered by asking Helene why she now wore dresses instead of the fisherman's trousers she had sported in Saint-Tropez—and whether that

was connected to the fact that the Prussian interior minister
and deputy Reich commissar 'Herr Bracht was also exercising
his influence in France to defend the honor of women'.[118] By
that point, Hasenclever was already unable to find a publisher
for his play about the Marseilles prostitute, and after only
three performances, following right-wing pressure, his and
Tucholsky's Columbus play was dropped from the repertoire
of the Leipzig Schauspielhaus.[119]

These were the experiences, context and atmosphere that
informed *Background for Love*, also written in the late summer of
1932. Helene worked quickly on the project. On 7th September
Wolff wrote to Marita Hasenclever: 'As I type this, Helene,
who sends her fond regards, is sitting in front of the house
and amusing herself by writing a lively work of prose from
this southern landscape called *Background for Love*. She finds it
uplifting and relaxing.'[120] Although superficially apolitical, the
novella contains a transnational, humanistic world view contrary to the spirit of the times and the prevailing relations of
power. The narrative is also, on the surface at least, completely
non-feminist—the woman in the story would never rebel or
insist upon her rights. But although Helene didn't question
traditional gender roles, she did turn them on their head. The
portrait of France, the 'drawing' of southern Europe, passes
back and forth between the wealthy older man and the penniless young woman as a 'gift' and perhaps, too, as an object
of negotiation. The France which the man presents with a
grandiose gesture represents liberation from the constraints and
gloom of their German homeland, but it also signifies excess,

cannot be inhabited in the long term and basically confirms the German stereotypes. The woman, who is all too well aware that her own 'reserves' can be exhausted, breaks out of her passive role, entering into an exchange with the 'background', the new environment, and transforming her shortcomings into surfeit and her material and social drawbacks into a cultural advantage by converting France into a moderate, simple, humane principle which the man also learns to comprehend in the end. Here, the man is no longer the creator and the woman no longer nature formed by him. The opposite is true. The man is nature, and the woman is able to shape and form him in the interest of a more cordial and humane mode of life.

'I know that things are going to get hard now' says the female narrator when they set off to return home. 'We'll go back to where we were, under a harsh sky, under a harsh law. Happiness is presumption, and it won't be so lightly pardoned there, even by the gods who give it as a gift.' Despite everything, Wolff and Helene didn't budge in their determination to return to Germany that fall and establish a life in Berlin. In late September they assembled their things and stored them away for the winter in the *cabanon*. But before actually setting off north they fulfilled the 'wish dearest to the hearts' of Wolff and Hasenclever to see Spain and northern Africa.[121] For six weeks, the three of them visited Saragossa, Madrid, Toledo, Córdoba and Sevilla, then took the ferry from Cádiz to Algeciras, spending a week in Marrakesh before returning via Casablanca and Fes from Algiers to Marseilles on 17th November. Subsequently Wolff and Helene traveled to Geneva and Zürich, where they splurged on a night in the city's best hotel, the Baur en Ville, before arriving in Berlin via Stuttgart and Dresden on 24th November.

The previous day, Hitler had rejected Reich President Hindenburg's call to form a parliamentary coalition and a new government. Instead, he demanded that Hindenburg allow him to constitute a government on his own with autocratic presidential powers. There was still considerable hesitation about such a violation of the German constitution, but conservative elites in Germany were becoming increasingly tempted to throw in their lot with the Nazis. If Wolff was to have any chance of procuring a position commensurate with his interests and needs, he was going to have to re-enter circles that overlapped with those elites which also contained liberal democrats.

In Berlin, he and Helene initially stayed with Countess Adelheid Kalckreuth, his ex-wife Elisabeth's sister. Immediately after their arrival in the German capital he was confronted with a social life whose tempo and intensity overshadowed even what he had been accustomed to in Munich. Female friends who lived in city—Princess Viola Reuss, Baroness Karoline von Gebsattel and above all Thea Dispeker, who was a director of the Central Institute for Education and Teaching in the Prussian Ministry of Culture—once again appeared in his journal. The same was true of Peter Reinhold, his former brother-in-law, who had bought his publishing house and who, as a former finance minister, German State Party deputy to the Reichstag, director of the *Vossische Zeitung* newspaper and industrialist, was extremely well connected. Wolff's revived circle also included

Erik-Ernst and Charlotte Schwabach, who had been among the main financiers of the Kurt Wolff Publishing House, heirs from banking families and art patrons and several publishers, including Knaur, Droemer and Rowohlt. He met Arnold Rechberg in the German Automobile Club, the journalist Friedrich Sieburg and his wife in the Kaiserhof Hotel, and the diplomat and philosopher Baron Gerhard von Mutius, along with others, at a gathering of the European Cultural Association. This list could go on. Wolff's life was again a continual series of concerts, teas, shopping and evening events. One particularly important figure was the enormously influential diplomat's wife, writer and niece of Hindenburg, Helene von Nostitz, whose salon was frequented by *tout Berlin*. She assembled artists and nonconformists like the acute, idiosyncratic social observer Count Harry Kessler, whose famous diaries mention many of Wolff's contacts at the time, as well as Hindenburg's fellow political travelers. There Wolff also met the wife of the later Nazi finance minister Hjalmar Schacht and Colonel General Hans von Seeckt, one of the founders of the Reichswehr. Less than a year later, in October 1933, Helene von Nostitz would be one of the eighty-eight writers who swore an 'oath of most loyal obedience' to Hitler.

Helene Mosel took no part in these circles. She continued to write, tried together with Marita to find a publisher and never felt at home in Berlin or indeed Germany. At Christmas she traveled alone to Munich to see her mother and her siblings. For the first time in more than two and a half years, she spent almost three weeks with them. Never before had she seen her sister

Liesel more than fleetingly since the latter was a child. As close and affectionate as her relations with her family were, the fact that her siblings at first didn't share the full extent of her revulsion at the Nazis and the political trend in Germany divided them. But she herself had 'grown old and less temperamental', and there's no indication of any serious quarrels.[122] Wolff spent Christmas in Fürstenberg with the Gebsattels before visiting his children and ex-wife in Munich, Elisabeth's brother Wilhelm Merck in Darmstadt and his father and stepmother in Bonn.

On 11th January 1933, he and Helene were reunited in Berlin. They moved into a boarding house, hunted for an apartment and still had high hopes for the future. Wolff had made connections with the legation counselor Johannes Sievers, the director of the visual art section of the cultural department of the German Foreign Ministry, who was an active supporter of Expressionism, although it was by then considered outdated. Sievers revered Wolff as *the* publisher of that cultural movement.[123] Sievers and a colleague named Hempel suggested Wolff put together a program commissioned by the Foreign Ministry for promoting German culture abroad—something like a predecessor to today's Goethe Institute.[124] Talks about the project proceeded positively. Helene also had prospects. John Holroyd Reece, whom Helene met in Berlin in mid-January without Wolff, commissioned a translation from her for 600 marks. And both the Ullstein and the Rowohlt publishing houses showed interest in her novella.

Then, on 30th January, Hindenburg agreed to make Hitler Reich chancellor. That morning Wolff wrote letters, and in the afternoon and evening he had four different appointments. In the days that followed, he and Helene listened to Hitler and the other Nazi leaders' speeches on the radio. By mid-February Hasenclever had already left Germany for Paris. Wolff and Helene moved into his furnished apartment in an artists' colony on Laubenheimer Square in the well-heeled Wilmersdorf district. The name on the doorbell was the Aryan-sounding one of Sigrid Engström, a former inhabitant, which, it was hoped, would prevent searches and harassment by gangs of SA. The day they moved in, Helene wrote to Georg:

> Kurt and I are very depressed. That's the reason for my extended silence, along with the translation in which I'm also absorbed. We are now surrounded by fascism, which makes my hair stand on end. It's shameful that this man represents Germany. Everything the government decrees is the purest barbarianism—surely you can't approve either. Or do you? We've finally gotten an apartment, Hasenclever's old one. He's now in Paris. It's small, cute and practical. I feel at home in it insofar as I can feel at home at all in today's Germany. I feel fairly composed about my future arrest for making unseemly remarks about the 'Führer' since I know I will not be able to keep my mouth shut forever. Forgive me for not yet having sent the books. Everything looks so grim that I no longer feel assured enough to spend any money.[125]

Every arrangement made between Wolff and the Foreign Ministry before 30th January was rescinded. Rumors swirled

that the Nazis were planning a bloodbath and night of reck-
oning to eliminate their enemies and satisfy their supporters'
desire to act upon their aggression. It was speculated that a
fake assassination attempt on Hitler would serve as the pretext
for unleashing violence. Many people were afraid and considered leaving Berlin, if only for southern Germany, before the
national election called for 5th March.[126] By 26th February
at the latest, Wolff and Helene decided to abandon Germany
again. On 1st March they saw their closest friends, the Sievers,
who had treated Wolff with 'warmth, trust, understanding and
friendship' in his bitterest days and to whom he would later
write that they had taken on 'an enormous significance, indeed,
forgive me, a significance beyond that of you as individuals'.
He explained: 'Your behavior toward me, which I experienced
immediately before my departure from my beloved homeland,
was infinitely uplifting, but it also made my departure more
terrible and painful. You will understand why I often think back
on these final experiences and occurrences and why they have
become, in conjunction with the two people I associate with
them, symbolic and almost impersonal.'[127] Wolff and Helene
also took their leave of Thea, Viola, Karoline and Marita.
They then boarded the night train for Aachen, reaching Paris
on 2nd March 1933.

Helene had sent her brother a package with some clothes
and a farewell letter on 26th February. The letter read:

Kurt and I have decided for various reasons to depart before
5th March—probably this Wednesday or Thursday. I often

think of your words: there's no room anymore for these sorts
of people. Kurt was offered a very interesting post, in which
he was also very interested, in the cultural department of the
Foreign Ministry (cultural propaganda for German art abroad
by arranging prestigious exhibitions, concerts, lectures and
theater evenings) and would almost certainly have gotten it,
when on 30th January only those who were members of the
Nazi Party were deemed eligible for official and semi-official
positions, and everything was cancelled. Cultural propaganda
is of course a joke when every time members of the government open their mouths, all that comes out is bloody froth.
What I have heard on the radio the last few days, criminal
harangues of the most nauseating sort by men like Göring,
Goebbels and their ilk, made one truly despair for the German
people. You can understand why people abroad are now
calling us Boches [a pejorative French term for Germans].

We are going for four weeks to London via Paris to resolve
some business that's still up in the air. Maybe we'll come back
here, but maybe we'll prefer to stay somewhere far away. I'm
sad and depressed. It's no fun feeling so homeless. At the start,
everything seemed to be coming together as easily as could
be expected, but since the Nazi Party dictatorship, there's
no room anymore for a person of character. I assume you
see things differently. I think of you a lot right now. I have
repeatedly reread the letter by your friend which you gave
me and I agree with him from the bottom of my heart. 'The
intoxication with the unreal weakens reality.' This seems to
be a primeval problem with German people. Reality isn't

enough for them, they don't adapt to the facts, and they end up throwing away life because it bores them. Because normal life is insufficient, they constantly create chaos and destruction. Today's Germany has become a powder keg capable of detonating the entire European world. And all because the Germans find it easier to die than to live.

What I hear, see and feel is mass intoxication, mass insanity, mass psychosis and a mood reminiscent of 1914. Maybe it will ebb in time, but it's bad enough that this atmosphere was possible in the first place... I have greatly admired Kurt throughout these days, which have brought nothing but disappointment. He has more backbone, more character, than I thought. He is submissive, but he doesn't compromise himself.

So until we see or hear from one another again... Let me give you the most emotional of hugs, your Helle.

Kurt and Helene married in London on 27th March and went via Paris and Montagnola to Ticino, Switzerland, where they would have liked to settle down near Hermann Hesse. But although they received residence permits that May, they were disappointed and put off by the 'not at all hospitable' atmosphere in that country.[128] Moreover, they failed to find suitable accommodation they could afford, so they returned after all to Saint-Tropez, taking up their former life in the *cabanon* and Villa Schlumberger, despite its lack of electricity and running water. As in the previous summer, it served as a guest house for Hasenclever and a rotating cast of friends and family. In September Helene went back to Munich for another three weeks. During that time she grew closer to her youngest sister—my grandmother—with whom, unlike Georg at that juncture, she was in complete political agreement and felt a common revulsion against 'today's Germany', which made her want to 'vomit with its cult of strength and violence, beyond any sense of justice'. She called it a 'prison, not a fatherland, a barracks worse than any under [Kaiser] Wilhelm, where at least only people's legs, not their minds and thoughts, were trained to march in military goosestep'.[129]

From that point on, Helene and her relatives would only ever see each other outside Germany. She and Kurt never returned to the Third Reich, although they seemed to be off the radar of the Nazi authorities, as Germans living abroad, and weren't persecuted as either racial or political enemies.[130] With the exception of Kurt's stepmother, who was considered partially Jewish under the Nuremberg Race Laws and who joined the Wolffs abroad in 1937, none of their family members, including Kurt's sister, children and ex-wife, suffered any notable persecution in Nazi Germany. Kurt and Helene were émigrés by choice, who could financially afford and emotionally bear to stay away from Germany. They didn't actively resist the Nazi state up until 1939. Instead, they did everything they could to live inconspicuously and in peace. But when forced to choose, they preferred 'backbone' and 'renunciation' to bad compromises. Kurt and Helene had their son Christian, who was born in Nice in 1934, registered as a French citizen. With that they clearly chose France over Germany, and there was no way back. In the summer of 1938, having lived in Italy for three

years, after the chaos of Hitler's visit to Mussolini but before
the introduction of anti-Semitic legislation, they applied for
French identification papers, which was tantamount to opting
out of German citizenship. 'You ask why I've requested *titres
de voyage* for Helene and myself,' Kurt wrote to Hasenclever on
11th August 1938. 'The answer is, thus far neither Helene nor
myself have been denied a (German) passport extension. But
I applied for the *titres* nonetheless. In part just in case. But also
because we no longer *want* a German passport—of course, I
will have to hand over our German passports when the *titres* are
issued. Some people may consider this course of action wrong-
headed. But I'm taking that risk and don't believe I'll regret
it.'[131] Up to that point they had generated some income, first
in France, then Italy, by taking in house guests from Germany,
most of them Jewish, who wanted to relax in a freer atmosphere.
Once German Jews in Italy were subject to deportation back to
Germany or required to emigrate, however, the basis of those
earnings was removed.

The Wolffs left their house in Italy and returned to Nice.
Money was running short. A period began that Helen Wolff
later remembered for its rising numbers of suicides. Concern,
particularly for their son, squeezed them 'like an ice-cold
ring'.[132] In 1939, thanks to Reece, who hired Helene to work
for the Albatross Press, they were able to move to Paris. Kurt,
too, found a job with a specialist mail-order antique bookseller.
When the war started, children in Paris were evacuated and
five-year-old Christian was sent to a boarding school in La
Rochelle. The Wolffs lived in an apartment on the Seine across

from Notre-Dame. Kurt Wolff was interned in the Stade de Colombes, together with all other male 'enemy aliens' from Germany, Austria, Hungary and the dissolved Czechoslovakia who were between seventeen and fifty years old. But he was released after a couple of days thanks to the intervention of influential French friends. In the hope for protection, but foremost out of loyalty to democratic France, the Wolffs volunteered to work for the German propaganda division of the French Ministry of Information, led by the writer and diplomat Jean Giraudoux. Helene composed several pamphlets aimed at mothers to be dropped by air over Germany.

In legal terms, their work for the propaganda division was treason against Germany. From then on, had they fallen into German hands, it would have meant their certain deaths. When Paris fell in June 1940 Kurt and Helene fled, spending weeks not knowing the other's whereabouts, Kurt on the move ahead of the Germans through Val d'Isère with a group of German émigrés who had released themselves from the internment camp at Chambaraud, Helene alone, from the Gurs internment camp in the Pyrenees. On 26th June Walter Hasenclever committed suicide in the Les Milles internment camp. With little more than the clothes on her back, and after spending several nights homeless on the road, Helene found shelter in a remote corner of Gascony. An Austrian countess, Berthe Colloredo, took her into her castle, a dilapidated fifteenth-century estate that was like something from a fairy tale. The two women became the closest of friends. Under Colloredo's protection, a motley community of refugees and émigrés of conscience from Nazi Germany worked the fields of the estate during the week. On Sundays they went to Mass. Helene read Lao-tzu under a chestnut tree. It wasn't until September that she and Kurt, who had managed to reach Nice in the meantime, succeeded in arranging for their son to be smuggled from occupied to unoccupied France. Once reunited in Nice, the family desperately began to apply for visas and travel papers to avoid becoming trapped as so many others were. They succeeded in getting themselves on the list of the Emergency Rescue Committee. Food was in short supply. The refugees weren't allowed to work, many were already going hungry. Those not lucky enough to be well connected faced being turned over to the murderous German authorities.

By early February 1941, the Wolffs had all their various visas: entry visas for the US, transit visas for Spain and Portugal and, perversely the most difficult to obtain, departure visas from France. The train trip to Madrid was uneventful, but the train to Lisbon was battered by a fierce storm, and when they arrived in the Portuguese capital their tickets for the passage to New York still had to be paid for. Kurt was forced to beg his friends in Switzerland for money. Christian had contracted whooping cough and Helene was running a fever by the time they boarded the *Serpa Pinto*, the Portuguese ship aboard which Kurt had secured a tiny cabin. The *Serpa Pinto* arrived in New York on 21st March. Thus the Wolffs had escaped to the New World, while the old one in Europe was going up in flames.[133]

What became of *Background for Love*? Despite the Nazis' rise to power, Rowohlt had agreed in April 1933 to publish Helene's story. But then came the book burnings, and the publishing house rescinded its offer. 'The gravity of the time doesn't allow them to,' Kurt Wolff wrote to Marita back in Germany. 'We're back where we were. And dear Helene has resigned herself to that for the moment.'[134] Ullstein had also rejected the manuscript because it was set in France. Nonetheless, *Background for Love* helped the Wolffs make connections without which they perhaps wouldn't have been able to save themselves by fleeing to the US.

In 1933, an editor at Ullstein had encouraged Helene not only to continue writing but to contact another publisher, who may well have been Emil Oprecht at Europa Verlag in Zürich.[135] Oprecht's estate in Zürich Central Library contains a typed manuscript of the novella that represents an alternative to the one the author kept in the rust-brown envelope, with different protagonists, an eleven-page excursus and another pseudonym, 'Susanne König' instead of 'Stefan Palm'.[136] The nationality of the German couple who travel to France was changed by hand to Swiss, references to the political situation in Germany in 1932 were deleted and the text was updated in places. In both typewritten manuscripts there is a reference to the 1935 Anglo-German Naval Agreement. In the summer of 1936, Helene, exhausted from accommodating guests, took five weeks' holiday in Zuoz, Switzerland. There, she had time to write and revised the novella, although not for Oprecht but for an English literary agent, Robert Klein, to whom Hasenclever had introduced her. Helene sent him the manuscript in September 1936, but nothing came of it.[137]

In the spring of 1939, the Wolffs, having moved to Paris, received a visit from Emil Oprecht.[138] He was a friend of Thomas Mann, and he and his wife Emmy did what they could from Switzerland to give pro-European, anti-nationalist writers and thinkers from Germany a platform and helped them in every possible way. The Wolffs gave Emil Oprecht manuscripts and brochures to take back with him to Zürich, including two copies of *Background for Love*.[139] To facilitate potential publication in Switzerland, Helene had made further changes to the narrative, transferring the action to the summer of 1938.

In this version, the summer of the Swiss couple in southern France in September 1938 is disrupted by the Munich Conference and the fears of imminent war. Amidst the general mobilization in France, the son of the farmer who rents the narrator the *cabanon* is called up. He takes his leave, giving a short speech intended to communicate the French situation to a Swiss readership. The speech evoked Swiss values to appeal to 'neutral' Switzerland, which by 1938 was swaying under German pressure, to reconsider and side with France after all. 'They [the Germans] thought we wouldn't march into battle, madame. They think the planet belongs to them because we love peace. The planet, madame, belongs to those who have patience. We French don't love marching off to battle, but we insist on justice. All people have a right to exist, not just the strong, and if the world is to live in peace, Herr Hitler must be more polite. His mother brought him up badly. If what is said is true, he never learnt anything of value. *C'est un homme sans métier*. How can he respect the work of other people?' After the now-Swiss narrator hears these words, she reflects on the French: 'Everything loud, violent and destructive is anathema to these people, who have become mature as they have grown civilized, who have gained in stature and see the meaning of life in its preservation. Should this world now be obsolete, die out and perish?' She then makes a comparison with the Swiss: 'Whether we are Swiss or French, something that seems more elevated than blood and race unites us in this September hour: the belief in moderation, value and the rule of law.' The world, she proposes, is divided into outlooks, not nations. 'We know just as well as they do what's at stake. For a long time and in vain, we Swiss believed we could be a model and example to the world, a prefiguration of what Europe could someday be. Until suddenly the talk turned to the "threat of the Swissification of Europe" in tones of contempt.' In a department store in Nice, the couple learn that, for the moment, peace has been preserved in Munich, and they experience French steadfastness and love of peace as people around them start spontaneously singing the 'Marseillaise'. Then they return to their little house, leaving the 'days of war' behind them: 'Something more important was going on here. The grapes were being harvested.'

Like many others, Helene Wolff was fooling herself concerning the prospects for peace in Europe. Four months after Oprecht's visit in Paris, Germany invaded Poland, shattering the illusions of Munich. Although Kurt Wolff was only interned as a German for a few days and the *Drôle de guerre*—the 'Phony War'—was not that noticeable in the French capital, the start of the Second World War basically removed any chance that

Helene's novella would be published in Switzerland. From that point on, Oprecht had to submit all manuscripts to Swiss Army censorship. Unfortunately, his correspondence with the censor concerning *Background for Love* wasn't preserved, but we do have the letters he sent on behalf of many other manuscripts. They show what 'neutrality' meant for Switzerland in that era. Nothing with even a hint of criticism of Nazi Germany, or a positive tendency toward France or anti-militarist or internationalist attitudes, was cleared for publication.[140]

Oprecht was unable to publish Helene's novella, but in early August 1940 he sent her a much-needed double advance, at which she was delighted.[141] The money didn't come, as she believed, from Oprecht's publishing house. It came from a fund for émigré German writers in France the Oprechts had put together from donations from their Swiss friends and acquaintances in Zürich after France's military defeat. The Oprechts tirelessly collected money and cooperated with the Emergency Rescue Committee in the US, Varian Fry and the Centre Américain de Secours in Marseilles, with Thomas Mann and the German author Hermann Kesten, Swiss aid organizations, a contact at the French embassy in Bern and many other people who tried to help save the lives of writers, publishers and intellectuals by allowing them to escape to America. US immigration quotas were long exhausted, and American borders were essentially closed to immigrants from Germany and Austria. Refugees hoping to enter the US had to get themselves added individually to the Emergency Rescue Committee's list.

Emil Oprecht repeatedly sent the Wolffs money in 1940 and 1941 and helped see to it that everything was done on both sides of the Atlantic to allow them to emigrate. In turn, Kurt Wolff sent Oprecht books from Nice and provided him with information about and contact with other refugees, whom the publisher also tried to help. The Oprechts' activism was not entirely selfless. They had their own names put on the list as well and procured visas in case Switzerland became fascist or was conquered by Nazi Germany.

In the meantime, in Nice, another opportunity emerged for *Background for Love* to see the light of day, albeit as a film, not a book. On 10th August 1940, Kurt Wolff wrote to Oprecht that all the 'aces' of French cinema had congregated in and around the city, and that he had made friends with a French director.[142] There was interest in Helene's story in film circles, Kurt claimed, and Oprecht was to send one of the manuscripts in his possession to Nice, even if that entailed a certain risk. In fact, the Wolffs did get back a manuscript, and in October 1940 Helene turned it into a film treatment.[143] But this too turned out to be a dead end, probably because the Vichy regime's Law on the Status of Jews of 3rd October and France's collaboration with Nazi Germany effectively killed off the French film scene.[144]

In March 1941, Helene brought the version of the manuscript Oprecht had returned with her to New York. In the nine months that followed, in which she and Kurt re-oriented themselves in America, and before the founding of Pantheon Books, which would become their life's work, Helene tried one final time to establish herself as a writer. She must have taken up the manuscript of *Background for Love* again, since she reversed almost all the changes and deleted the compromises she had made in the interest of getting the novella published in Switzerland. The Swiss couple were once again Germans, and the story was transported back to 1932 from 1938—although on a few occasions she overlooked anachronisms such as the reference to the 1935 Anglo-German Naval Agreement.

Helen Wolff was probably not exceedingly bothered that the story was never published in the US. She was at least as happy with her life as a publisher as she would have been with that of an author. She no longer needed to write. And she was willing to let posterity describe how everything had turned out as it did, as long as posterity stuck to the truth.

'At my death, burn or throw away unread!'

Thanks to Christian Wolff, Holly Nash Wolff, Alexander Wolff, Jon Baumhauer, Maike Albath, the Wolff, Mosel, Steinbeis and Vorwerk families, the Beinecke Rare Book and Manuscript Library, the Rare Book and Manuscript Library at Columbia University, the Deutsche Literaturarchiv Marbach and the Zentralbibliothek Zürich.

NOTES

1   Herbert Mitgang, 'Profiles: Helen Wolff', *The New Yorker*, 2nd August 1982, pp. 41–73, here 73.

2   She carefully edited the posthumous volumes of correspondence and material issued under Kurt's name, which rarely mentioned her and, if so, only in the margins. See Kurt Wolff, *Autoren, Bücher, Abenteuer. Betrachtungen und Erinnerungen eines Verlegers*, Berlin, no date (1965); Bernhard Zeller and Ellen Otten (eds), *Kurt Wolff. Briefwechsel eines Verlegers 1911–1963*, Frankfurt/M, 1966, expanded edn Frankfurt/M, 1980; Wolfram Göbel, 'Der Kurt Wolff Verlag 1913–1930', Archiv für Geschichte des Buchwesens, Vol. 15/3, pp. 522–962 and Vol. 16/6, pp. 1299–455, Frankfurt/M, 1976 and 1977, reprint Munich 2007; Steven J. Schuyler, 'Kurt Wolff and Hermann Broch: Publisher and Author in Exile' (thesis at the Department of Germanic Languages and Literature, Harvard University), Cambridge/Mass, 1984. Helen Wolff's correspondence with Wolfram Göbel and Steven Schuyler shows how adroit she was at using concerns for 'privacy' to withhold certain information from the public. See Helen and Kurt Wolff Papers, Beinecke Rare Book and Manuscript Library, YCGL MSS 16, Box 8 Folder 333 and Box 39 Folder 1219.

3   Günter Grass, 'Nachruf auf Helen Wolff, vorgetragen in Leipzig am 30. April 1994', in *Johnson-Jahrbuch 2* (1995), pp. 13–18, and Daniela Hermes (ed.), *Günter Grass/Helen Wolff, Briefe 1959–1994*, Göttingen, 2003, p. 433.

4   See Mitgang, 'Profiles: Helen Wolff'.

5   The rust-brown envelope also contains a fragmentary German-language narrative entitled 'The Mother', probably part of a projected novel about her childhood in the Balkans. It was published in 2007 in the literary journal *Sinn und Form* (Vol. 2, pp. 149–56).

6   Maria Stadelmayer to Kurt and Helen Wolff, 5th May 1962, Christian Wolff private papers.

7   The correspondence, including letters to the German embassy in Constantinople, is part of the Mosel/Steinbeis/Vorwerk family papers.

8   Information provided by telephone (28th July 2007) by Hedwig 'Mausi' Theisen, née Reisinger, the daughter of the director at the time, who along with my grandmother was another girl accepted by the school. Helene's report cards are kept in the archive of Landheim Schondorf.

9 Helene's passion for literature so impressed Edine Philippi, the twelve-year-old daughter of IG Farben board member Richard Philippi, that Edine's own daughter, the literary critic Verena Auffermann, called her career the 'direct consequence' of Helene's influence and characterized herself as 'one of what are surely your many secret daughters'; Verena Auffermann to Helen Wolff, 4th February 1994, Helen and Kurt Wolff Papers, Beinecke Rare Book and Manuscript Library, YCGL MSS 16, Series IX, Box 98, Folder 3042; interview with Verena Auffermann, 10th March 2007.

10 Helene Mosel to her mother, no date (Easter 1924), Mosel/Steinbeis/Vorwerk family papers.

11 On the history of Kurt Wolff's German and European publishing houses see Wolfram Göbel, 'Der Kurt Wolff Verlag 1913–1930', Archiv für Geschichte des Buchwesens, Vol. 15/3, pp. 522–962 and Vol. 16/6, pp. 1299–1455, Frankfurt/M, 1976 and 1977, reprinted unchanged Munich 2007; Barbara Weidle (ed.), *Kurt Wolff. Ein Literat und Gentleman*, Bonn 2007.

12 Roth started an at the time unprecedented bidding war at the time between Kurt Wolff and a half-dozen other publishers. See David Bronsen, *Joseph Roth. Biographie*, Cologne 1974, p. 306.

13 In 1947 Helen Wolff drew a comparison between the atmosphere at Pantheon Books and the Kurt Wolff Verlag: 'All in all, a much better, freer tone prevails than at the old K.W.V. People don't tremble as much before the head of the house, and the head of the house isn't betrayed as often by the cowardice of his underlings.' Helen Wolff to Liesel Steinbeis, 18th November 1947, Mosel/Steinbeis/Vorwerk family papers.

14 The results of the investigation by a detective named Sydney A. Musson can be found in the Helen and Kurt Wolff Papers, Beinecke Rare Book and Manuscript Library, YCGL MSS 16, Box 30, Folder 918–21; Helene summarized them in two texts: 'J.H.R.—Sein Leben von ihm selbst erzählt' and 'Sein Leben in der Wirklichkeit'.

15 Kurt Wolff to Hans Mardersteig, 6th March 1931, at a point when he had burnt the 'final external bridge' with Pantheon Casa Editrice; Helen and Kurt Wolff Papers, Beinecke Rare Book and Manuscript Library, YCGL MSS 16, Series IX, Box 96, Folder 2961.

16 On this score, there are a good dozen letters from her mother to Georg in 1929–30; Mosel/Steinbeis/Vorwerk family papers.

17 Helene Wolff to Liesel Mosel, 13th November 1935; Mosel/Steinbeis/Vorwerk family papers.

18 Kurt Wolff to Hans Mardersteig, 22nd March 1929, Helen and Kurt Wolff Papers, Beinecke Rare Book and Manuscript Library, YCGL MSS 16, Series IX, Box 96, Folder 2961.

19 Interviews with Nikolaus Wolff, May/June 2006.

20 Josephine Mosel to Georg, 5th November 1928, Mosel/Steinbeis/Vorwerk family papers.

21 Josephine Mosel to Georg, 28th April 1929, Mosel/Steinbeis/Vorwerk family papers.

22 Helene Mosel to Georg, no date (April 1931), Mosel/Steinbeis/Vorwerk family papers.

23 Josephine Mosel to Georg, 1st and 22nd June and 5th and 7th July 1929, Mosel/Steinbeis/Vorwerk family papers.

24 Probably a 1928 Buick sedan.

25 Helene Mosel to Georg, 5th September 1930, Mosel/Steinbeis/Vorwerk family papers.

26 Friedrich Sieburg, *Gott in Frankreich? Ein Versuch*, Frankfurt 1929. The German title played on the idiom 'leben wie der Herrgott in Frankreich' (literally 'living like God in France', or living the high life).

27 Helene Mosel to Georg, 4th March 1930, Mosel/Steinbeis/Vorwerk family papers.

28 Helene Mosel to Georg, 25th March 1930, Mosel/Steinbeis/Vorwerk family papers.

29 See Kurt Wolff's journal, Christian Wolff private papers.

30 Helene Mosel to Georg, 4th June 1930, Mosel/Steinbeis/Vorwerk family papers.

31 Helene Mosel to Georg, 25th March 1930, Mosel/Steinbeis/Vorwerk family papers.

32 Thirty years later, Kurt Wolff would recall this time in a letter to the art historian Ernst Gombrich on 26th February 1962, Helen and Kurt Wolff Papers, Beinecke Rare Book and Manuscript Library, YCGL MSS 16, Box 8, Folder 338.

33 Kurt Wolff was once accused of defamation for openly discussing the homoerotic implications of George's idea of education. See Thomas Karlauf, *Stefan George. Die Entdeckung des Charisma*, Munich, 2007, p. 366; Lothar Helbing and C. V. Bock (eds), *Stefan George. Dokumente seiner Wirkung. Aus dem Friedrich Gundolf Archiv der Universität London*, Amsterdam,1974, p. 284.

34 Helene Wolff to Georg, 14th November 1934, Mosel/Steinbeis/Vorwerk family papers.

35 Helene Wolff to Liesel, 15th December 1935, Mosel/Steinbeis/Vorwerk family papers.

36 Helene Wolff to Georg, 16th January 1934, Mosel/Steinbeis/Vorwerk family papers.

37 See Guido Müller, *Europäische Gesellschaftsbeziehungen nach dem Ersten Weltkrieg: Das Deutsch-Französische Studienkomitee und der Europäische Kulturbund*, Munich 2005.

38 Ibid., p. 340.

39 Kurt Wolff to Helene Mosel, 16th April 1930, Christian Wolff private papers.

40 Kurt Wolff to Helene, 22nd/23rd and 23rd/24th April 1930, Christian Wolff private papers.

41 Kurt Wolff to Helene, no date (postmarked 26 April 1930), Christian Wolff private papers.

42 Josephine Mosel to Georg, 17th May 1930, Mosel/Steinbeis/Vorwerk family papers.

43 Ena Mosel to Georg, 17th May 1930, Mosel/Steinbeis/Vorwerk family papers.

44 Kurt Wolff to Hans Mardersteig, 13th May 1930, Helen and Kurt Wolff Papers, Beinecke Rare Book and Manuscript Library, YCGL MSS 16, Series IX, Box 96, Folder 2961.

45 Helene Mosel to Georg, 4th June 1930, Mosel/Steinbeis/Vorwerk family papers.

46 Franz Werfel to Kurt Wolff, 25th March 1930, in *Kurt Wolff: Briefwechsel eines Verlegers 1911–1963*, Frankfurt/M, 1980, pp. 349–51.

47 Helene Mosel to Georg, 5th September 1930, Mosel/Steinbeis/Vorwerk family papers.

48 Ibid.

49 Helene Mosel to Georg, 28th July 1930, Mosel/Steinbeis/Vorwerk family papers.

50 Helene Mosel to Georg, 12th October 1930, Mosel/Steinbeis/Vorwerk family papers.

51 'Möglichkeiten und Grenzen der Gemeinschaft', in *Die Musikpflege. Monatsschrift für Musikerziehung, Musikorganisation und Chorgesangswesen*, Leipzig, 1930, pp. 177–90; also in *Jugendführung*, Düsseldorf, 1930, 8/9 (special issue), pp. 289–99, and multiple reprints in various Guardini compilations until 1975.

52 Ibid., pp. 64f.

53 Ibid., p. 81.

54 Helene Mosel to Georg, 12th October 1930, Mosel/Steinbeis/Vorwerk family papers.

55   Helene Mosel to Georg, 16th June 1931, Mosel/Steinbeis/Vorwerk family papers.

56   The title of Guardini's essay closely resembles that of the sociologist Helmuth Plessner's 1924 classic *Die Grenzen der Gemeinschaft* (*The Limits of Community*).

57   Kurt Wolff to Hans Mardersteig, 6th March 1931, Helen and Kurt Wolff Papers, Beinecke Rare Book and Manuscript Library, YCGL MSS 16, Series IX, Box 96, Folder 2961.

58   Helene Mosel to Georg, 16th November 1930, Mosel/Steinbeis/Vorwerk family papers.

59   Helene Mosel to Georg, no date (1931), Mosel/Steinbeis/Vorwerk family papers.

60   Helene Mosel to Georg, 2nd March 1931, Mosel/Steinbeis/Vorwerk family papers.

61   Helene Mosel to Georg, no date (early 1932), Mosel/Steinbeis/Vorwerk family papers.

62   Kurt Wolff to Marita Hasenclever, 18th December 1931, Kurt Wolff Archive, Beinecke Rare Book and Manuscript Library, YCGL MSS 3, Box 4, Folder 125.

63   Kurt Wolff to Hans Mardersteig, 24th July 1931, Helen and Kurt Wolff Papers, Beinecke Rare Book and Manuscript Library, YCGL MSS 16, Series IX, Box 96, Folder 2961.

64   Helene Mosel to Georg, 16th June 1931, Mosel/Steinbeis/Vorwerk family papers.

65   Helene Mosel to Georg, 21st July 1931, Mosel/Steinbeis/Vorwerk family papers.

66   Ibid.

67   Walter Hasenclever to Kurt Wolff, 21st July 1931, Kurt Wolff Archive, Beinecke Rare Book and Manuscript Library, YCGL MSS 3, Box 4, Folder 124.

68   Kurt Wolff to Hasenclever, 6th October 1931, ibid.

69   Helene Mosel to Hans Mardersteig, 24th February 1932, Helen and Kurt Wolff Papers, Beinecke Rare Book and Manuscript Library, YCGL MSS 16, Series IX, Box 96, Folder 2961.

70   Ibid.

71   Walter Hasenclever to Kurt Wolff, 17th September 1931, Kurt Wolff Archive, Beinecke Rare Book and Manuscript Library, YCGL MSS 3, Box 4, Folder 124.

72   Johannes von Kalckreuth to Hasenclever, no date, Kurt Wolff Archive, Beinecke Rare Book and Manuscript Library, YCGL MSS 3, Box 4, Folder 133.

73 Kurt Wolff to Walter Hasenclever, 23rd September 1931, Kurt Wolff Archive, Beinecke Rare Book and Manuscript Library, YCGL MSS 3, Box 4, Folder 124.

74 Kurt Wolff to Walter Hasenclever, 19th May 1931, Kurt Wolff Archive, Beinecke Rare Book and Manuscript Library, YCGL MSS 3, Box 4, Folder 123.

75 Magali Nieradka-Steiner, *Exil unter Palmen. Deutsche Emigranten in Sanary-sur-Mer*, Tübingen, 2018; Jeanpierre Guindon, 'Sanary-sur-Mer, capitale mondiale de la littérature allemande', in Jacques Grandjonc and Theresia Grundtner, *Zone d'ombres 1933–1944. Exil et internement d'Allemands et d'Autrichiens dans le sud-est de la France*, Aix-en-Provence, 1990, pp. 25–33.

76 Helene Mosel to Walter Hasenclever, 26th November 1931, Kurt Wolff Archive, Beinecke Rare Book and Manuscript Library, YCGL MSS 3, Box 4, Folder 124.

77 Helene Mosel to Hans Mardersteig, 3rd December 1931, Helen and Kurt Wolff Papers, Beinecke Rare Book and Manuscript Library, YCGL MSS 16, Series IX, Box 96, Folder 2961.

78 Kurt Wolff to Walter Hasenclever, 26th November 1931, Kurt Wolff Archive, Beinecke Rare Book and Manuscript Library, YCGL MSS 3, Box 4, Folder 124.

79 Kurt Wolff to Hans Mardersteig, 22nd October 1931, Helen and Kurt Wolff Papers, Beinecke Rare Book and Manuscript Library, YCGL MSS 16, Series IX, Box 96, Folder 2961.

80 Carl von Ossietzky was charged with treason and betrayal of military secrets. He was sentenced in November 1931 to eighteen months' imprisonment.

81 Kurt Wolff and Helene Mosel to Walter Hasenclever, 26th November 1931, Kurt Wolff Archive, Beinecke Rare Book and Manuscript Library, YCGL MSS 3, Box 4, Folder 124.

82 Walter Hasenclever to Kurt Wolff and Helene Mosel, 1st December 1931, ibid.

83 Kurt Wolff to Hans Mardersteig, 23rd December 1931, Helen and Kurt Wolff Papers, Beinecke Rare Book and Manuscript Library, YCGL MSS 16, Series IX, Box 96, Folder 2961.

84 Helene Mosel to Georg, 23rd December 1931, Mosel/Steinbeis/Vorwerk family papers.

85 Helene Mosel to Georg, no date (early 1932), Mosel/Steinbeis/Vorwerk family papers.

86 Ibid.

87 Helene Mosel to Walter Hasenclever, 26th November 1931, Kurt Wolff Archive, Beinecke Rare Book and Manuscript Library, YCGL MSS 3, Box 4, Folder 124.

88 Helene Mosel to Hans Mardersteig, 31st December 1931, Helen and Kurt Wolff Papers, Beinecke Rare Book and Manuscript Library, YCGL MSS 16, Series IX, Box 96, Folder 2961.

89 Helen Wolff to Christina Fischer, 2nd February 1992, Helen and Kurt Wolff Papers, Beinecke Rare Book and Manuscript Library, YCGL MSS 16, Series IX, Box 98, Folder 3042.

90 Claire Goll to Yvan Goll, 4th February 1932, Barbara Glauert-Hesse, 'Nachwort', in Claire Goll, *Arsenik / Eine Deutsche in Paris*, Göttingen, 2005, p. 273.

91 Walter Hasenclever to Kurt Wolff, 11th January 1932, Kurt Wolff Archive, Beinecke Rare Book and Manuscript Library, YCGL MSS 3, Box 4, Folder 126.

92 Helene Mosel to Hans Mardersteig, 24th February 1932, Helen and Kurt Wolff Papers, Beinecke Rare Book and Manuscript Library, YCGL MSS 16, Series IX, Box 96, Folder 2961.

93 Ibid.

94 Kurt Wolff to Walter Hasenclever, 4th June 1931, Kurt Wolff Archive, Beinecke Rare Book and Manuscript Library, YCGL MSS 3, Box 4, Folder 123.

95 Walter Hasenclever to Kurt Wolff, 12th June 1931, ibid.

96 Walter Hasenclever to Kurt Wolff, 21st June 1931, Kurt Wolff Archive, Beinecke Rare Book and Manuscript Library, YCGL MSS 3, Box 4, Folder 124.

97 Helene Mosel to Georg, 21st July 1931, Mosel/Steinbeis/Vorwerk family papers.

98 Helene Mosel to Georg, 30th September 1931, Mosel/Steinbeis/Vorwerk family papers.

99 Helene Mosel to Marita Hasenclever, 26th November 1931, Kurt Wolff Archive, Beinecke Rare Book and Manuscript Library, YCGL MSS 3, Box 4, Folder 125.

100 Kurt Wolff to Marita Hasenclever, 18th December 1931, ibid.

101 Friedrich Voit, *Karl Wolfskehl. Leben und Werk im Exil*, Göttingen, 2005, p. 74.

102 Karl Wolfskehl to Helene Mosel, 31st December 1931, Helen and Kurt Wolff Papers, Beinecke Rare Book and Manuscript Library, YCGL MSS 16, Series IX, Box 98, Folder 3039.

103 Marita Hasenclever to Kurt Wolff, 6th April 1932, with a copy of the letter from the Deutsche Verlagsanstalt, Kurt Wolff Archive, Beinecke Rare Book and Manuscript Library, YCGL MSS 3, Box 4, Folder 126.

104 Kurt Wolff to Hans Mardersteig, 26th November 1931, Helen and Kurt Wolff Papers, Beinecke Rare Book and Manuscript Library, YCGL MSS 16, Series IX, Box 96, Folder 2961.

105 The first book to appear with the new publishing house was *Dubliners* by James Joyce. In 1932, Reece and Wegner spontaneously founded the Odyssey Press to publish Joyce's *Ulysses*, which because of its alleged obscenity hadn't appeared at all in Britain and only in abridged form in the US.

106 Bert Kasties, *Walter Hasenclever. Eine Biographie der deutschen Moderne*, Tübingen, 1994, pp. 290–93.

107 Gerda Schairer, 'Der Dichter Walter Hasenclever', unpublished manuscript, Deutsches Literaturarchiv Marbach, cited in Kurt Tucholsky, *Gesammelte Werke*, Vol. 3: 1929–1932, Hamburg, 1967, Commentary B 388, p. 752.

108 René Schickele to Kurt Wolff, 17th August 1932, Kurt Wolff to René Schickele, 31st August 1932, Kurt Wolff Archive, Beinecke Rare Book and Manuscript Library, YCGL MSS 3, Box 7, Folder 271. See also Hans Wysling and Cornelia Bernini (eds), 'Jahre des Unmuts. Thomas Manns Briefwechsel mit René Schickele 1930–1940', *Thomas-Mann-Studien*, Vol. 10, Frankfurt/M, 1992, p. 217, footnote 7.

109 *Kurt Wolff. Briefwechsel eines Verlegers 1911–1963*, Frankfurt/M, 1966, expanded edn Frankfurt/M, 1980, p. 272.

110 Kurt Wolff to Marita Hasenclever, 23rd July 1932, Kurt Wolff Archive, Beinecke Rare Book and Manuscript Library, YCGL MSS 3, Box 4, Folder 127.

111 Helene Mosel to Georg, 25th July 1932, Christian Wolff private papers.

112 Helene Mosel to Georg, no date (early 1932), Mosel/Steinbeis/Vorwerk family papers.

113 Helene Mosel to Georg, 27th May 1932, Mosel/Steinbeis/Vorwerk family papers.

114 See the letters by Kurt Wolff, Marita Hasenclever and Lilly Ackermann in June/July 1932, Kurt Wolff Archive, Beinecke Rare Book and Manuscript Library, YCGL MSS 3, Box 4, Folder 127.

115 See Konrad Dussel, *Deutsche Rundfunkgeschichte*, Konstanz, 2004, pp. 75–80.

116 Walter Hasenclever to Kurt Wolff, 14th September 1932, Kurt Wolff Archive, Beinecke Rare Book and Manuscript Library, YCGL MSS 3, Box 4, Folder 127.

117 Kurt Wolff to Marita Hasenclever, 23rd July 1932, ibid.

118 Marita Hasenclever to Kurt Wolff and Helene Mosel, 18th August 1932, ibid.

119 Kurt Tucholsky, *Gesammelte Werke*, Vol. 3: 1929–1932, Hamburg, 1967, Commentary B 408, p. 769, and B 404, p. 766.

120 Kurt Wolff to Marita Hasenclever, 7th September 1932, Kurt Wolff Archive, Beinecke Rare Book and Manuscript Library, YCGL MSS 3, Box 4, Folder 127.

121 Helene Mosel to Georg, no date (September 1932), Mosel/Steinbeis/ Vorwerk family papers.

122 Helene Mosel to Georg, 13th December 1932, Mosel/Steinbeis/Vorwerk family papers.

123 Christian Saehrendt, *'Die Brücke' zwischen Staatskunst und Verfemung. Expressionistische Kunst als Politikum in der Weimarer Republik, im 'Dritten Reich' und im Kalten Krieg*, Stuttgart, 2005, p. 43.

124 Kurt Wolff to the Sievers, who visited him in exile in Italy, on 18th August 1937, Deutsches Literaturarchiv Marbach, A: Sievers, 70.129.

125 Helene Mosel to Georg, 17th February 1933, Mosel/Steinbeis/Vorwerk family papers.

126 See Kessler's diary entries between 20th and 28th February 1933, Harry Graf Kessler, *Das Tagebuch 1880–1937*, Bd. 9: 1926–1937, ed. by Sabine Gruber, Roland S. Kamzelak and Ulrich Ott, Stuttgart, 2010.

127 Kurt Wolff to the Sievers, 18th August 1937, Deutsches Literaturarchiv Marbach, A: Sievers, 70.129.

128 Kurt Wolff to Frans Masereel, 7th May 1933, Kurt Wolff Archive, Beinecke Rare Book and Manuscript Library, YCGL MSS 3, Box 6 Folder 214.

129 Helene Wolff to Georg, 16th January 1934, Mosel/Steinbeis/Vorwerk family papers.

130 In 1937, Liesel organized documents proving Aryan heritage for Helene though not for their 'quarter-Jewish' mother. Kurt also tried to get the baptism documents of his grandparents but then gave up on it. His Jewish forefathers had converted to Christianity two generations previously. After the early death of his mother Maria, née Marx, his gentile father married her sister Luise. Their father, i.e. Kurt's maternal grandfather, the mine director and railroad entrepreneur August Carl Ludwig Marx, had converted from Judaism to Protestantism in 1837 at the age of fifteen. Wolff's Jewish origins were diluted enough to not seriously affect his sister and his children in Germany, but in his case, they, together with his past as a publisher of many Jewish authors, certainly would have exposed him to not only political but also anti-Semitic persecution.

131 Kurt Wolff to Hasenclever, 11th August 1938, Deutsches Literaturarchiv Marbach, A: Hasenclever Neuzugang.

132 Kurt Wolff to Ena Mosel, who was by that point living with Georg in Chile, 2nd March 1939, Mosel/Steinbeis/Vorwerk family papers.

133 See Sylvia Asmus and Brita Eckert, 'Emigration und Neubeginn. Die Akte "Kurt Wolff" im Archiv des Emergency Rescue Committee', in Barbara Weidle (ed.), *Kurt Wolff. Ein Literat und Gentleman*, Bonn, 2007.

134 Kurt Wolff to Marita Hasenclever, 3rd June 1933, Kurt Wolff Archive, Beinecke Rare Book and Manuscript Library, YCGL MSS 3, Box 4 Folder 130.

135 Helene Wolff to Georg, 7th August 1933, Mosel/Steinbeis/Vorwerk family papers.

136 Zentralbibliothek Zürich, Verlagsarchiv Oprecht/Europa-Verlag, Ms. Oprecht, T 203.

137 See the correspondence between Kurt Wolff and Walter Hasenclever in September 1936, Deutsches Literaturarchiv Marbach, A: Hasenclever Neuzugang.

138 Kurt Wolff to Walter Hasenclever, 6th May 1939, ibid.

139 Helene Wolff to Emil Oprecht, 31st July 1940, Zentralbibliothek Zürich, Verlagsarchiv Oprecht/Europa-Verlag, Ms. Oprecht, 10.16.

140 See the correspondence between Helene Wolff and Emil Oprecht in July and August 1940, ibid. Almost all the manuscripts Oprecht submitted at the time were rejected, so it may be that he never tried his luck with *Background for Love*. See, for example, Ms. Oprecht 13.1 and 13.32.

141 Helen Wolff to Georg and Ena Mosel, no date (August or September 1940), Mosel/Steinbeis/Vorwerk family papers.

142 Helene Wolff to Kurt Wolff, 25th July 1940, Christian Wolff family papers. There is no saying for sure who Kurt's 'friend in the film business' was. It could be that someone from the circles around Jean Renoir showed interest in *Background for Love* in Nice.

143 Kurt Wolff to Emil Oprecht, 21st October 1940, Zentralbibliothek Zürich, Verlagsarchiv Oprecht/Europa-Verlag, Ms. Oprecht, 10.16.

144 Jean Renoir also emigrated to the US around the same time as the Wolffs.